Beautiful Fury

By Katharine E. Hamilton

ISBN-10: 0-692-06825-2
ISBN-13: 978-0-692-06825-0

Beautiful Fury

www.katharinehamilton.com

Cover Design by Kerry Prater.

To my sister, Kerry.
For understanding my creative quirks and
helping make them beautiful.

Acknowledgments

Thanks to my family. It's easy to do what you love when you have people who support and love you.

Thanks to my alpha and beta reader teams. MK, Macy, Kerry, and Wellborn. Love that I can count on you guys each and every time to not only read my rough drafts, but to give me honest feedback.

Thanks to my editor, Lauren Hanson. I love that no matter your changes, you are still able to capture my voice and style.

And thanks to my readers. You guys are amazing. I love meeting you, hearing from you, and writing for you. Thank you.

« CHAPTER ONE »

Running a palm down the intricately woven tapestry, Caroline Pritchard allowed the image of Native American women gathered around the loom to filter through her mind; diligent hands threading, pulling, and pushing threads together to create what she considered a masterpiece, but what they, she envisioned, considered a necessity without flare. The detail was exquisite and expertly crafted. The colors vibrant. The patterns complex. The woven textile hung beautifully against the cream adobe wall inside the gallery, and she lifted a hand to adjust the small light fixture hanging above it.

"Looks good, Ms. Caroline." Ed, the gallery's maintenance manager, nodded her direction as he mopped the front foyer. "Real spiffy. I think the people are going to love it."

"Thanks, Ed." Caroline smiled as she stepped back to survey her spotlight adjustment. "I'm having a hard time walking away from it."

"Can't make it look any better than you have already, Ms. Caroline. I think the artist will be mighty pleased with your work."

"Let us hope so," Caroline muttered softly under her breath as she waved a farewell to Ed and made her way back to her office.

She needed this showcase to go well. Not just for her sake, but for the gallery's. Santa Fe, New Mexico, was the hottest spot in the country for art, and she had landed her dream job of managing a gallery on Canyon Road, the illustrious half-mile of pavement, where over one hundred galleries, studios, jewelers, boutiques, and restaurants crowded together to create an indulgent shopping experience for tourists and locals to bask in the beautiful artistry of the city. Nestled in the foothills of the Sangre de Cristo Mountains, Canyon Road provided picturesque surroundings that enticed its visitors to capture some of that beauty for themselves, and shoppers from around the country flocked to Santa Fe to grasp hold of a small portion of its beauty. She hoped her work at Daulton's Gallery convinced them to choose Daulton's selection of beauty; that amongst all the galleries, tourists would find hers special.

Native American art was tricky to showcase on Canyon Road. Mainly, because though its beauty was undeniable, it was also fairly common. It was, after all, what Santa Fe was most known for. But Caroline hoped to bring her knowledge and expertise to Daulton's and make their particular pieces stand out amongst the other galleries. Her knack for creative display and eye catching presentation had previously earned her a position at the National Gallery of Art in Washington D.C. And though she loved the capitol city, she wanted a change. *And a challenge*, she realized. Santa Fe had always been on her list of potential job targets, and it was not until last year that she finally made the move. Taking what she learned in D.C.— the ability to showcase multiple styles of work to a broad audience— Caroline aimed to bring a fresh approach to the Daulton that would help the gallery stand out amongst its neighbors. Finding local and talented artists were on the top of her list, and so far she had maintained the gallery's success, but had yet to bring anything new to the table.

Feeling discouraged and slightly disappointed in herself, she decided this next art show needed to be a unique approach to displaying Native American art. Unique enough that it drew people inside the gallery and made them want to purchase the pieces for their own homes. "One can only hope," she whispered, as she nudged a magazine aside. Her eye landed on a small pop of color on the bottom corner of the cover. She lifted the magazine and stared at the beautiful sculpture gracing a wooden table in front of broad sweeping windows, the sun radiating through the bold colored glass and casting rainbows about the room. *Beautiful.* She flipped open the pages and turned towards the designated page to learn the artist's name, but no name was listed. Huffing a frustrated breath, she turned back to the front of the quarterly and attempted to find the cover's photograph details. Nothing. *Why feature a piece of art on the cover of an art magazine and not list the artist?* Perplexed, she typed in 'local glass artists Santa Fe' into her computer's search engine and waited. Maybe she could track the artist down with a little bit of sleuthing. She flipped through the remaining pages of the magazine and did not see another piece even closely related with the cover image. *Odd.*

Her search results pulled up on the monitor and she clicked through various sites until she landed upon a brief snippet about a local artist with the initials of F.W. A few snapshots of the work produced by F.W. proved he or she was the artist Caroline was looking for. However, the only glimpses of his or her glass art were several pieces privately sold or from small boutiques around the city. *Why was it not displayed in a gallery?* She felt the sudden rush of enthusiasm that only comes from brilliant ideas that set the mind afire as she began searching more on F.W. and the gorgeous glass pieces created by their crafty hands. This was the artist she needed. This was the artist that would set Daulton's Gallery apart from the rest. Now she only needed to find them.

∞

Sweat trickled down the center of his back as he slowly turned the pipe with his left hand, his right making the appropriate snips and pulls to form the shape he desired. He was accustomed to the heat, the endless perspiration, and the ache of sore muscles from his toil. They all contributed to the art he loved. Today, however, he felt sloppy and clumsy. After breaking one piece during his first transfer of the day, he eyed the disappointing, shattered pieces littering the floor. Finnegan Walsh held fast to the pipe so as not to repeat the same mistake. Transferring from blow pipe to punty and the separation of pipe and punty was the moment in a piece that required a delicate touch. Though working with glass in itself was a delicate art, there were some movements that required his full focus and attention. This moment, that deep breath before the plunge, had his back stiffening and his capable hands working swiftly. He rapped the blow pipe, the pipe successfully breaking away and the molten glass attaching to the punty. He then rolled his chair quickly over to the glory hole and stuck the gathered glass into the fire to reheat. Constant heat and motion were a necessity in every piece, and though his arms and hands cramped from time to time, the labor produced such beauty that he pushed his limbs to the limit.

Finn's eyes darted to the clock on the wall before he removed the punty from the glory hole and rolled back to his work bench. He made quick work of opening the piece up to create the mouth of what would be a fluted vase. Not just an ordinary vase, but an elegantly tall and delicate vase that might grace the table of a parlor or foyer, a focal piece for whomever wished to purchase it. He'd worked hard to achieve the right colors. The reds and oranges shot up the base much as his flames acted in the furnace; a statement piece to be sure.

Satisfied with his work, he then tapped the punty against the work bench, the vase dropping away and landing into a large box filled with a fire blanket. Slipping on his Kevlar gloves, Finn lifted the piece and carried it to the annealing oven where it would slowly cool over the next fourteen hours. He prayed it survived and did not crack during the cooling process. He needed a win today after his shattered first attempt.

He released his breath, never realizing he held it during the transfer, and sighed as he removed his gloves and ran his hands through his dark, in-need-of-a-cut hair. A throat cleared and had him jumping in his tracks before annoyance took hold. "No one is allowed in my workshop," he barked before turning. His eyes landed upon his sister's amused smirk as she crossed her arms and leaned against the door.

"I waited, didn't I?"

"You know I don't like people coming to my shop. Why are you here?"

"Someone's in a mood this morning." She surveyed his tense shoulders and the glass pieces sparkling the floor. He reached for a broom and began quick work of sweeping up the mess. "Guess you had a mishap this morning?"

"Obviously. Now what do you want?"

"Geez, Finn, you could at least seem glad to see me just a smidgen. I usually bring good news. For the most part. Well, not all the time. But today I do." She grinned that cheeky smile that always melted his reserve and had him motioning to a set of stools. "I'll grab us a drink." He pulled two cans of soda from a small refrigerator and tossed her one. "I'm listening."

Used to her brother's gruff personality, Rory never skipped a beat. "The amber sculpture sold. The one from Mary Ann's shop. It sold." She slipped a check from her shirt pocket and handed it to him. His eyes widened at the amount. "No need to thank me." Her smile broadened and turned into a small laugh as she spun in a circle on the rotating stool.

"How?" Finn rubbed a hand over his stubbled face and looked at his sister in awe. "Why?"

"Why? Because it was a beautiful piece, Finn."

"Well, yeah, I know that. But why so much?"

"Maybe because your little sis knows the value of your work. You underestimate your skill. Plus, I have requests from several boutiques who also wish to showcase a few of your pieces. So... you better get to working." She winked as she took a long, satisfying sip of the soda.

"I don't rush my work, Rory, you know that."

"I know. That's why I have not committed to any of them yet. I specifically told them I would speak to the artist and see if he wishes to contribute."

Finn slipped the check into his back pant pocket and stood, tossing his empty soda can into the trash as he walked towards a large oak cabinet. He pulled a key out of his pocket and unlocked the padlock. Swinging open the doors, he looked at her. "Pick what you want."

Rory stood in surprise. "Since when have you started hiding pieces under lock and key?"

"Only the ones that are special to me." Finn pointed. "These are also some of my larger pieces. So if you're going to need some statement pieces to sell, this is where you choose. Otherwise, stick to the shelves." He motioned towards the floor to ceiling shelves that lined the entire shop, the different shapes and colors gracing the space catching the eye. "I'll pull from the shelves first, and if I feel like I need a larger piece I'll come to you." Rory could see Finn was not ready to part with anything from his cabinet. That was evident as he stood, arms crossed, a firm frown etched over his face. She saw the slight relief wash over his features before he made his way back to his work bench.

"Is that all you needed?"

"Um, no, actually. Mary Ann said a gallery manager has been asking about you. Apparently she's approached several of the shop owners that feature your work."

"And?" He began organizing his bench, putting away tools and supplies he no longer needed and bringing new ones to the table.

"And it sounds like she's wanting to commission you for an art showcase at her gallery."

"I don't do shows."

"I know, but-"

"No buts." The finality of his tone had her back straightening and her temper starting to flare.

"You don't even want to hear what she is offering?"

"No."

Huffing in frustration, Rory stomped towards him as he continued working without glancing up. "People love your work, Finn. Right now, I've shucked off several shops that want to display more of your work. You could be making more money. Your pieces are valued far higher than either of us imagined. And as much as I hate to say it, you're in demand."

He smirked at that but continued to ignore her.

"Fine. I'll just tell everyone you do not wish to sell anymore pieces and you can just hoard them in your cupboards until you're old and gray. And then when you die, I'll sell them all. They'll probably be even more valuable then any way." She crossed her arms in a defiant pout as he looked up. His steely blue eyes softened a brief moment before he tossed a tool onto the table.

"I do not want to stop selling pieces, Rory. I just don't want to be commercialized. Plus, I do not create on demand. I create as inspiration strikes. Preparing for an art exhibit requires multiple pieces. Pieces that the gallery manager oversees and decides which to showcase. If he or she does not like certain pieces, then the request for more comes in. I do not produce based on their needs. I produce based on mine."

"I know." She slid back onto the stool. "I just feel like one show won't kill you. Besides, afterwards, you can start being picky again and your pieces would be a rare find for people. The thrill is in the hunt, as they say."

He laughed at that and her response was a smug smile. "Think about it. As of right now, she still does not know much about you other than your initials. Mainly because *no one* knows much about you. All people know is that I'm your representative. You're mysterious, Finn. And mystery sells. Think about it."

She stood and gave him a quick peck on his cheek. "Now go shower. You smell." And with that, Rory darted out the door and left him contemplating the check in his pocket and the potential of more to come.

∞

Caroline stepped out of the small boutique and shut the door behind her, the finality of the gesture putting an official close on the dead end search for the elusive artist known as F.W. All the shops and boutiques that sold his work had no clue as to his official name. The fact she found out the artist was indeed a man was one small success, but she found it hard to celebrate that matter when all the shop owners only dealt with a female. Not one, *not one* had a business card to give her, and now she stuffed the folded magazine cover into her purse. Defeated for the day, she made her way up the street to the quaint bistro on the corner. After endless hours of searching around the city for clues on F.W., she deserved a pick-me-up, and Frank's chocolate cake was nothing if not a morale booster. One slice was all she needed and then she'd be on her way home for the afternoon to rest until the gallery's exhibit of the Native American pieces began later that evening.

Frank's wife, Matilda, offered a wave in greeting and immediately set about slicing a piece of cake for Caroline. Caroline made her way to the outdoor patio and sat at a small wrought iron table nestled amongst potted columbine, sand verbena, fendler's sundrops, and overhanging ferns, the scent of the local flora teasing her senses. Matilda made her way towards the table and slid into the seat opposite Caroline. Matilda's face held warmth, as much from the exertion of working behind the counter as from her personality. The woman was a joy, and Caroline accepted her motherly clucking just as all her other customer's did. "That kind of day?" she asked, wiping her hands on the tips of her apron. Her portly body shifted in the wrought iron chair as she attempted to find a comfortable position.

"Yes. I'm hoping to end it on a good note." Caroline slid the cake in front of her and lifted her fork. "Thank you for this."

"Of course. I could just tell you needed it when you walked inside. Now tell me what happened today to have you in such a slouch."

Sighing, Caroline offered a weak smile. "I have given myself an impossible task, and yet, I still feel completely disappointed in myself for failing. Why did I bother?"

"Okay," Matilda reached across the table and squeezed her hand. "Tell me what impossible task you hoped to accomplish today."

Taking a small bite from her cake, Caroline contemplated how to express her utter disgust with her lack of success when Matilda quickly rose, rushed inside the patio doors and almost immediately returned with a peach Bellini. "To wash it down." She said, as she leaned forward on her elbows. "Now tell me."

Caroline took a quick sip of the refreshing drink and began retelling her day's journey throughout the city seeking out all the distributors of F.W.'s artwork. "I mean, I understand the artist wanting privacy, but it's almost as if he doesn't exist." Caroline vented. "The only interaction everyone had in regards to him was through a woman, but yet, none could tell me for sure what her name was because it had "been so long" since they'd last seen her. So here I sit, wondering if I should keep trying."

"Never give up, dear," Matilda said with a light chuckle as she surveyed Caroline's annoyed glance. "Perhaps you were just looking in the wrong shops, hm?" She slapped her hands on the table. "Come with me." Standing, she waited until

Caroline stood and placed her napkin next to her plate. She then led her through the bistro doors and through the swinging door to the kitchen. Once inside, the smells of roasting meat and vegetables made Caroline's mouth water and while her senses were reeling from the tantalizing smells, Matilda shoved her through a narrow doorway into a tiny office off the kitchen. She flicked on the light and pointed.

Caroline gasped. Before her sat a stunning crystal bowl with a deep purple center, the brilliant colors covered mostly with peppermint and butterscotch candies. A candy dish. Matilda and Frank possessed one of the most beautiful pieces she'd seen all day and they used it as a glorified candy dish. The irony made Caroline suppress a laugh, but she could not stop her fingers from lightly rubbing over the rim of the bowl. "Where did you get this?"

"From the artist himself." Matilda said proudly.

Stunned, Caroline turned towards her. "Seriously?"

"Well it's here, isn't it?" Matilda replied.

"Do you know him?"

"I do. Since he was a boy. His parents were good friends of mine and Frank's before they moved to Taos. Our kids grew up together."

Caroline's eyes sparkled as she beamed towards Matilda. "Matilda," hope resounded in her voice as a small squeal escaped her lips and she grabbed the woman's hands in thanks.

"Now, don't get too excited, dear. I won't give you his name."

Confused, Caroline straightened. "Why not?"

"Because I would never hear the end of it, and I know how he appreciates his privacy."

"But you can tell me how to contact him?"

"I believe I can." Matilda answered with a smile.

She reached towards her desk and grabbed a sticky note. "This here is Rory's number. She handles all his affairs. Just contact her with what you're after and I'm sure she can help you out."

"Oh, Matilda!" Caroline jumped at the woman and gripped her in a big hug. "Thank you, thank you, thank you."

Matilda giggled as Caroline slowly released her. "You're welcome. Now if you do meet him, I was not the one who pointed you his direction, you hear? He would never forgive me."

Frowning, Caroline looked at her friend. "I don't want to put you in a difficult situation, Matilda."

"As long as you stick with Rory, you won't."

"Are you positive?" Caroline held the sticky note towards her.

Matilda nudged it back towards Caroline. "I'm sure. I've seen what you've done at the Daulton, Caroline. I know you will showcase whatever art comes your way with respect and courtesy. And I will admit, I am rooting for you on this one. If anyone can get F-" She trailed off as she realized she almost said the artist's name and then grinned. "Well, if anyone can do it, it's you. Best of luck, dear."

Caroline hugged her once more and made her way back to her table to finish her cake and Bellini. She stared at the yellow note and fished into her purse to grab her cell phone. Dialing the number, she waited as the phone rang two times before voicemail clicked on. "You've reached Rory Graves, you know what to do." A beep sounded and Caroline fumbled with what to say. She hadn't thought that far ahead. "Um, hello, this is Caroline Pritchard. I am, well, I am the gallery manager at Daulton's Gallery in Santa Fe, New Mexico. I was told you were the point of contact for an artist with the initials F.W. I would like to discuss some exhibition opportunities or acquisition possibilities of his glass work." She rattled off her phone number and hung up.

She exhaled loudly as she laid her phone on the table and stared at it. Now she had to wait.

Patience was not her strong suit, and something told her F.W. would require an enormous amount of patience.

«CHAPTER TWO»

Finn counted himself a patient man when it came to life. After all, glassblowing required tons of it, but as he listened to his sister spout off about the recent message she received, he found his patience slowly ebbing away until the glower on his face reflected his mood. "I do not do shows, Rory. You know this. End of discussion." He huffed past her, his shoulder slightly bumping her as he made his way out of his shop and across the worn path between the outbuilding and his house. The cabin style home sat amongst the beautiful backdrop of mountains and national forest, secluded and remote, exactly how Finn preferred to live. The picturesque scenery provided inspiration and peace, two things he could not live without. He did not classify himself as a complete hermit, but the thought of people, groups of people, wandering amongst his glass and asking him questions made his stomach curl into knots. He avoided people as best he could. Other than Rory and her husband, Dan, his parents were the only other interaction he really had. And he liked it that way. People were too nosy, or false, or pretentious. And no one could value his work as much he did himself.

"I think it is worth discussing." Rory sent a pleading look to Dan as he stepped towards Finn.

"Think about it, Finn," Dan began, but was silenced by the heated glare Finn shot his way. He turned towards Rory, "I tried, honey." He shot Finn a quick grin as Rory threw up her hands and groaned. "You two are going to send me to an early grave," she spouted at their retreating backs. Finn offered a slap on Dan's shoulder as he and his childhood friend made their way towards the house and the grill that sat on an open deck. Finn reached into a cooler and tossed Dan a beer before opening his own.

Rory clomped up the deck stairs and fisted her hands on her hips. "This conversation is not over. I will meet with the gallery manager and at least hear what she has to say. I think it is time you start thinking bigger, Finn. You have an entire workshop full of amazing pieces just sitting there collecting dust. It's time we do something with them."

Dan looked at his wife and then back to her brother. He waited as he started to see the rising tempers in each of them and knew a face-off was about to commence. He took a long swig of his beer and braced himself.

Finn turned from the grill, raw meat in hand as he glowered at his sister. "I said, no, Rory. It is my work. If I say no, you cannot show or sell it. That's final."

"No, not final. You asked me to promote your work. Well, that's what I'm doing. How am I to promote your work if you do not let me? No wonder your last two reps quit. You're impossible."

"They quit because the only other choice was them being fired," Finn growled. "They were thieves."

"Well, I'm not. I only have your best interests at heart."

"Oh really?" Finn motioned towards Dan. "So you are not just wanting to push my pieces to earn more money so you can add onto your house?"

Rory stiffened and shot a quick glance towards Dan, who diverted his gaze immediately to the tree line behind her. "This has nothing to do with my house plans, Finn. The point is you would make money."

"And you receive commission," Finn pointed out. "Therefore, so would you."

"That's how business works!" Exasperated, Rory threw up her hands. "And what little I do make off your work goes towards my living expenses, yes. That's the point of a job. And whether or not Dan and I want to add onto the house is our business. Keeping your house is yours. I'm trying to help you earn a living so you can do that."

"I make a living just fine on the few pieces I sell here and there."

Rory walked to the table and sat, defeat in her shoulders, as she rested her chin in her hands and watched her brother place steaks on the grill. "Finn, honestly, have you not ever thought about having more? That your work is worth more than you give it credit for? Art is for sharing. You can't hoard it. It's not fair to others."

"I don't care about other people," Finn stated, no heat to his voice, and Rory knew that was true. Other than her and their parents, Finn did not share his heart towards others. Except Dan. *Sometimes,* she thought. Her brother had always lived alone, just him and his glass. And what little interaction with the outside world he had was just quick trips to town for supplies.

"Maybe it is time you started thinking of others," Dan cut in and held up his hands in peace as Finn spun around in surprise at his friend's interjection.

"Just because you're married to my sister does not mean you can take her side," Finn retorted, partly in jest, and partly in aggravation.

"I think, Finn," Dan continued, "if you saw how people appreciated your work, how it moves them, you would be more willing to expand your distribution."

"My art is for me, it does not matter to me how other people feel about it."

"Yes it does," Rory added. "You're just scared."

"Not scared," Finn stated on a sigh. "I'm tiring of this conversation. And since you are two of the four people I actually do tolerate in my life, I would like to somewhat enjoy our evening together."

"Fine. I'll drop it for now. But I'm still going to contact the gallery manager and hear her out. Who knows, maybe one of my other clients could benefit from her expertise."

"Other clients?" Finn turned while placing a steak on a plate and handing it to Dan. "What other clients?"

Rory stood and grabbed a plate as well and walked towards her brother. "Well, you can't expect to be my only client. Like you said, I have to make money too. And if you aren't selling your work, I don't get paid, so yeah, I have two new clients."

"What kind of art?"

"None of your business," Rory stated, as she grabbed the tongs from his hand and helped herself to her own steak before it passed from medium rare to well as he just stood there in shock. "You cannot expect me to wait around forever for you to decide when to let one piece out of your clutches, do you? One piece of art does not pay the bills, Finn."

Finn pondered that a moment and noticed that Dan reached across the table and squeezed Rory's hand. Money had never been a problem for the Walsh siblings. Their mother and father had done well in their own art dealings in the past and some of that wealth had filtered to their children. When his parents retired and moved further into Taos, he took over their house, his childhood home, and Rory moved into Santa Fe when she married Dan. Finn earned enough to maintain his home and land comfortably, and what little money trickled down from his parents sat in an account for the future, whatever it may hold. Rory received the same, but something had fixed worry on his sister's face as she and Dan sat quietly cutting into their steaks. Something she wasn't telling him. He wouldn't push now, not in front of Dan on the off chance it was a sore subject in regards to his income as well. Though Finn could not recall either of the two having trouble with work recently. He shrugged and made his way to the table. "Fine. Talk to her. I may be willing to part with a couple pieces."

Surprise flooded over Rory's face as a wide smile split across it. She gave him a quick side hug before turning back to her plate. "I promise I will not agree to anything unless I feel she is a good fit."

"Only a couple pieces, Rory. I will not do a show."

"Of course," Rory agreed, though inwardly she plotted how she could convince her brother otherwise.

∞

Caroline rubbed her fingers over her tired eyes. The Native American Exhibition went successfully the night before with the largest turn out to date, and for that she was grateful. But she could not help feeling frustrated that she had yet to hear back from Rory Graves. Her biggest lead looked as if it were about to be a dead end.

"Looks awfully empty in here." Ed popped his head through her office doorway and grinned. "That's always a good sign. You have a good show, Ms. Caroline?"

She offered a tired smile. "Yes, Ed, thank you. The purchased pieces have already been moved to the back room for shipping or pick up."

"Guess you better start finding some art to fill these empty spaces, hm?" He chuckled at her weary expression. "I'm just kidding. If you need me to help move some of the staple pieces back onto the floor, you just let me know."

"I will, Ed. Thank you."

He briefly nodded and stepped out, the sound of his broom swishing across the floor all she heard as she lifted the purchase tickets from the previous night to carry them to shipment. As she stood from her chair, the telephone rang and had her slowly taking a deep breath in order to sound chipper. "Good morning, Daulton Gallery."

"Hello, I am calling for a Caroline Pritchard, please."

"This is she." Caroline slowly sank back into her chair and grabbed a notepad and pen just in case.

"Hi, this is Rory Graves. I am returning your call."

Caroline bolted in her seat and leaned into the receiver. "Yes!" She tried to contain her excitement. "Yes, I'm so glad. Hello, Ms. Graves."

"Mrs.," Rory corrected, but in a friendly manner. "I am calling about the artist you wished to discuss."

"Yes, F.W. has been quite elusive for me, I am hoping you can shed some light on him."

"Of course, I will be on Canyon Road this morning meeting with a few clients. Would you like to meet for an early lunch?"

Caroline tried to tamper down her squeal of excitement as she eagerly agreed to meet at Frank's Bistro at eleven. Hanging up the phone, she jumped to her feet with a happy shout and dance before grabbing her tickets and making her way towards shipment with a new pep to her step. She had thirty minutes to kill and then she'd continue her hunt for F.W. in earnest.

By eleven, Caroline had managed to slip out of the gallery and make her way down the street to Frank's, praying the entire time that her meeting with Rory would go well; that possibly F.W. would be willing to showcase some of his glass work at her gallery. Ideas of displays swirled in her head and her heart raced along with her excited steps as she turned into the Bistro. Matilda waved and tilted her head to survey Caroline's mood before pointing to the menu board above her head. Obviously Caroline's mood had improved from the previous day or Matilda would already be slicing a piece of cake. That, Caroline decided, was a good sign in and of itself. "Hi, Matilda."

"Caroline," she greeted warmly, her hands on her plump hips. "I see you have that beautiful smile back."

"All thanks to you," Caroline admitted. "I'm here to meet Rory Graves." The slight shrill of anticipation at the end of the name made Matilda laugh.

"Then you are right on time," she pointed to a woman in her mid-twenties sitting at the same table Caroline occupied the day before and smiled. The woman's jet black hair caught the gleams of the sun and Caroline noticed deep streaks of purple mixed in. The short and choppy hairstyle framed her petite face well, and the purple amongst the black gave her an air of strength and just a little bit of spunk.

"Wish me luck," Caroline whispered, as she walked towards the table. "Mrs. Graves?"

Rory looked up, her lips splitting into a friendly smile as she stood. "Yes, Ms. Pritchard?"

"That'd be me." Caroline shook her hand and both women sat. "Thank you so much for meeting with me."

"Of course. I don't receive many calls in regards to F.W., so I will admit my curiosity was piqued."

"Really? That surprises me. His work is—" she paused, realizing no words could adequately describe the beauty of his work. "Breathtaking, and yet I still feel that word does not do him justice."

Rory laughed. "I agree, though I won't tell him that."

Matilda walked up and placed a sandwich in front of Rory and looked to Caroline. "And you?" She pointed to the menu in Caroline's hand.

"Oh, um, just the club, Matilda. Thank you." She watched her leave and then turned back to Rory who took a hearty bite from her sandwich, harboring no qualms about professionalism as a pickle slipped from the breading and dangled from her lips before falling to the plate. She grabbed her napkin and dabbed her lips on a laugh. "Sorry, not only am I starving, but Frank's food isn't exactly the most glamorous to eat."

Caroline smiled. "No worries."

"So what is it you are after with F.W.?" Rory asked.

"Well, a name for one." Caroline explained. "But I also would love to showcase his work. See, I'm pretty new to the Daulton Gallery, and we have yet to venture into new territory in regards to the art we exhibit. Canyon Road is known for its art, its unique exhibitions. I have yet to see anyone display a glass artist, and I would like to be the first. I saw this," she removed the magazine cover page that remained folded in her purse and spread it on the table. "This piece is gorgeous, and I have searched high and low for anyone who might know the artist. To be honest, I was sitting in this exact spot yesterday feeling quite defeated when

Matilda shared with me her crystal bowl and your number."

Rory ran her fingers over the worn creases of the page before her and looked into the eager but honest, green eyes of Caroline Pritchard. *A woman on a mission,* she thought. But an honest woman, and she liked what she saw. "And what's this?" She pointed to a small dark spot on the page and Caroline blushed. "That would be chocolate cake. I did mention I was drowning my defeat in Frank's cake, right?"

Rory hooted with laughter as she looked Caroline up and down. "Love it. And I like you. Now tell me what you have in mind."

Beaming, Caroline pulled several sketches from her portfolio and laid them out before Rory, pointing to certain rooms of the gallery and her plan for each one, all depending on what type of pieces F.W. provided, of course. But her overall concept was impressive. Her attention to detail, lighting, both natural and staged, showed Rory that Caroline Pritchard knew how to showcase her brother's work, and do it beautifully.

"And that is pretty much the gist of it," Caroline finished. "The night of the exhibit would be a cocktail hour, essentially. F.W. would be available to the patrons to answer questions about his pieces or just to put a face with the art. People love meeting the artist. And-"

Rory cut her off with a raised hand. "Yes, so that is where I will need to stop you. I may be able to commit a couple of pieces, but an entire show and an appearance are out of the question."

Deflated, Caroline's shoulders sank, but her professionalism forced her to try and hide her disappointment. Rory saw through her, though, and she reached for the sketches. "Though maybe I could try and convince him. Mind if I take these to show him?"

"Please do, and if he has any questions, tell him he can call me any time. Or if he wishes to tour the gallery beforehand, I do not mind showing him around."

"That won't be necessary. He will not leave his workshop." Annoyance laced Rory's words and she immediately cleared her throat to mask it. "I will just show him these and we can go from there."

"Thank you, Mrs. Graves."

"Just call me Rory." Rory grinned. "Mrs. Graves sounds too much like a teacher. Though my husband is a professor at the Santa Fe University of Art and Design, so I guess it is fitting."

"Wow, so art just seems to be a part of who you are." Caroline, impressed by her new contact, took a bite of her sandwich.

"Oh yes." She grinned. "My parents were antiquity dealers, mostly Native American pieces, naturally." She waved her hand around the area meaning to encompass Santa Fe. "My brother-" she trailed off quickly.

"Your brother?" Caroline asked, not noticing the slip up and glancing her direction as she ate.

"He's an artist," Rory said nonchalantly. "And my husband an art professor. So yes, art seems to take up the majority of my life."

"I could think of nothing better." Caroline grinned as she motioned towards her cake covered magazine page.

Rory laughed as she laid her napkin on the table and Matilda quickly came and swept her plate away.

"If you need to be back at work, please do not hesitate on my account." Caroline slipped a chip into her mouth and waited.

"Oh no, you are fine. I'm a fast eater. My brother accuses me of inhaling my food rather than tasting it." Her face softened at the mention of her brother.

"Is he your younger brother?"

Rory shook her head. "Older, though sometimes he acts younger."

"Men," Caroline teased and had Rory laughing once more.

Her face sobered a moment and she leaned forward as if taking Caroline in her confidence. "Ms. Pritchard,"

"Caroline, please."

A flash of a smile crossed Rory's face as she continued. "Caroline, I will be honest with you. F.W. is my most temperamental client. He does not do public appearances. He values his privacy more than most anything."

"So he's a hermit?" Caroline jested.

"Yes."

Caroline's smile faded as she saw Rory was perfectly serious. "Oh."

"And he's a stereotypical one at that. He despises social situations."

"It always surprises me how some people can live life without interaction or relationship. Well, that is assuming he isn't married, but still. Our relationships shape us into who we are. I cannot imagine not having that."

Rory's smile softened. "Yes, well, he's not married, and at the rate he's going, he never will be. I just wanted to explain who you're dealing with a bit so you do not raise your hopes too high."

"Maybe if I met him, he would see I am easy to work with?"

"I doubt I could even arrange that." The idea perked Rory up in her seat, though. Scheduling a meeting between the pretty blonde and her cantankerous brother would be impossible, but ambushing her brother with a surprise meeting... that might be just what he needs. "You know what? What are you doing tomorrow?"

"Just working at the gallery."

"Want to take a drive?"

Caroline's brows rose.

"Maybe a meeting with F.W. *is* what needs to happen. I can take you there and we can both discuss with him this opportunity."

Caroline nodded. "That would be wonderful. Thank you, Rory. I am sure once he sees the plans and hears from me personally, maybe he will feel more comfortable with the idea."

"I'm sure of it," Rory agreed, her smile widening as she thought of ensnaring her brother in a meeting with Caroline. Sometimes a giant push is what he needed, she assured herself. Sometimes it was up to her to nudge him in the right direction, little sister or not. And when faced with a beautiful woman who wore her emotions on her face, she just knew Finn had to be more likely to cave. Caroline Pritchard was just the shake up her brother needed.

«CHAPTER THREE»

Finn slipped his goggles over his face as he reached for his blow pipe. He'd wrestled all night with inspiration for this piece such that it took his aching back's extreme coercion to keep him in bed until this morning. Those few hours of extra rest did his body wonders as he stretched, lifting the blow pipe over his head and then rolling his shoulders. He walked towards the furnace and reached inside with the pipe to gather the melted glass he would need to begin his work. The music in his shop ran on autopilot, the classical riffs and crescendos keeping him focused while also providing its own stimulation as he worked. He heard a light scraping noise and felt his hackles rise as he knew someone had stepped into his shop. He couldn't stop to yell at the intruder, however, because he'd gathered his glass and must continue in his work until he reached a stopping point. He moved quickly to roll the glass on the marver to slowly shape it. He walked back to the glory hole and heated the glass again, his hands constantly turning the pipe. Removing the piece he walked back to the table and rolled the glass again. Constant movement requiring strength and patience as he walked once more to the glory hole.

He spotted movement out of the corner of his eye as his intruder stepped closer. Anger bubbled beneath his chest as he despised the invasion of his workshop but also his work space. He did not like feeling crowded. He needed room to breathe, to work. He needed them to leave. Without glancing up, he aimed his words towards the door. "No one allowed in my workshop! Leave!" He shouted above the music but also with extra force so as to issue his first warning. If it was Rory or Dan, they knew better. If it was his parents swinging by on a brief visit on their way to Angel Fire, he'd allow it, but would also make his frustration known in the meantime. Either way, he felt rushed. Glassblowing could not be rushed.

He moved the reheated piece to his table and began rolling it in pieces of frit. This particular frit was chosen to bring color to the piece and add depth to what he hoped would turn out to be a luminous sculpture for his parent's weekend home in Angel Fire.

He then walked back towards the glory hole. Constant reheating of the glass required multiple trips to the furnace. Maintaining the correct temperature as he worked was crucial in forming the glass. His music stopped and he heard the shuffle of feet as he pulled his piece from the hole and walked back to his table. His eyes caught a glimpse of his sister, immediate annoyance crossing his features. He noticed another figure towards the door, but did not glance that direction so as to stay focused on his task. More than likely it was Dan, and both of them knew they'd best prepare themselves for a tongue lashing.

He took a long breath and puffed into the blow pipe to begin expanding the piece. Slow, quick breaths bringing air into the glass and allowing the shape to continue to come forth.

"I come in peace," Rory announced, walking forward, knowing he could not respond when he was puffing into the pipe. "When you reach a stopping point, we need to talk."

The urgency in her tone had him looking up at her as she stood on the other side of his table. He saw the wonder in her gaze and he softened. He knew it was mesmerizing to watch a glassblower at work. After all, that is how he himself was first introduced to what would eventually become his career, his passion, and his obsession.

His first encounter with glass was when he was eight years old. His parents had taken him and

Rory with them on one of their art acquisition trips and Finn witnessed the art of glassblowing first hand. It would not be until ten years later that he would venture to Toledo to study the art and then go on to spend two years in Europe learning his craft. He loved that it took not only a creative mind, but the skill to match it: science when it came to the chemicals needed to make various adjustments to the glass and its color. The stubbornness not to give up on a piece no matter how many times you fail. And the wonder— the wonder of taking an unformed gathering of molten glass and turning it into something beautiful. That was where the magic lay.

"Back up, Rory," he commanded, but not in annoyance, merely out of necessity as he reached forward and grabbed the punty. As he began the transition from pipe to punty, another figure appeared next to Rory causing him to briefly glance up. Stunned by a stranger standing in his workshop, and the admiration in her beautiful green eyes, his hands slipped. He watched in horror as the piece fell to the floor and shattered. Livid, he whipped off his glasses and threw them on the table. "Who are you and what are you doing in my shop?"

∞

Remorse flooded Caroline's gaze as she stared at the broken shards scattered across the floor. She fumbled over what to say as his fiery blue eyes burned through her and the man's fury restrained itself merely by his grip on the edge of his table. Rory placed a supportive hand on Caroline's shoulder. "It was my fault, Finn. I brought Caroline in to see you work. I should have asked." Not feeling remotely sorry, Rory smiled smugly as Finn narrowed his gaze at her. She sensed his self-control start to return as he straightened and slowly released his grip on the table. "What are you doing here, Rory?" He stepped over the glass and made his way for the broom, his back to the beautiful stranger with his sister as he swept.

"I came to introduce you to Caroline. She's..." trailing off, she wracked her brain for a proper term so as not to be booted out immediately. "A friend." She looked at Caroline and winked so she would play along.

"Friend or no friend," Finn dumped the glass into the trash and faced them. "No one is allowed in my shop."

"Oh, calm down." Rory waved away his annoyance and nudged Caroline towards him. She saw her brother eye the woman with guarded interest. "Caroline, please meet my brother, Finn Walsh." She stressed his name so Caroline would understand that F.W. was the man before her. As if Caroline had not figured it out herself. Surprise lit her face as she turned towards Rory. "Your brother?"

Finn squinted at her comment and placed his hands on his hips. "I thought you said she was your friend?"

"She is," Rory said.

"Then why is she surprised I am your brother? Did you not tell her she would be meeting *your brother*?"

He was on to her, but Rory held firm while Caroline wanted little more than to crawl under his table and hide from those piercing eyes that showed nothing but disgust and repulsion.

"It's nice to meet you, Mr. Walsh." Caroline extended her hand and Finn ignored it. He turned and stormed out of his shop leaving Caroline gaping after him and an infuriated Rory hot on his heels.

She heard raised voices coming from outside as she stood awkwardly folding her hands in front of her. She risked glancing about his shop. The shelves lined with his glass pieces were stunning and she could not help but run a finger over the curve of a vase, the tanzanite blue achingly pure and flawless.

"Don't touch that." The command had her jumping, her hand bumping the piece and had her stepping forward to stabilize it. Two strong hands reached forward, a shoulder bumping her and causing her hands to shift over and bump the piece next to it. She gasped as she reached for it as well, praying the chain reaction would stop there. She saw Finn's hand reach for the other piece as well and hold, both glass works teetering to a still. "Now back away." Caroline obeyed immediately. When he turned, apologies poured from her lips as she began shrinking away from his rage. She backed into the door of the shop and paused a moment to readjust her feet before stepping out of the shop back into the yard. He followed, his presence filling the doorway, broad shoulders over a narrow waist, fists on his hips. He looked as if he could shoot up into the air at any moment and rescue the world from bad guys rather than being the nemesis himself. "I truly do apologize, Mr. Walsh. Your work is... exquisite." She felt herself rambling as she felt another hand fall on her shoulder. She jumped at the touch and relaxed when she saw it was Rory. "Don't let him scare you, Caroline. He's all talk." She smiled wickedly at her brother as he stepped out the door and shut it with force.

"Why are you here?" he asked Caroline. "And I want the truth."

She darted a quick glance at Rory and his sister nodded.

"I manage the Daulton Gallery in Santa Fe." She'd barely finished the sentence before he'd begun stomping his way towards his house. Appalled by his abrupt dismissal, Caroline stood in complete bafflement. She turned to Rory for guidance and only received a shrug. Shock and frustration washed over. She did not come this far to meet F.W. to only have him walk away from her. Sheer determination had her tramping towards the house. She followed his movements, climbing the deck stairs to the back entrance versus walking towards the front door out of politeness. He entered through a glass sliding door and turned to see her reach the top step before sliding it closed right in her face. He moved further into the house intending to ignore her yet underestimating her tenacity. She slid the door open and stepped inside, following the sounds of banging cabinet doors and the clattering of pots and pans. When she stepped into the kitchen, he did not turn around. "You know not to bring anyone here, Rory. I don't care what gallery or museum she's from, I don't care what her name is or who she is, she-" he paused as he turned and saw it was Caroline who graced his kitchen and not Rory. "You just came into my house?" His question was almost a whisper as he stood in stunned surprise.

"That's right." Caroline stepped closer and noted his taking a step back. *Good,* she thought, *she had him nervous now. Good.* "Mr. Walsh, my name is Caroline Pritchard, and I'm with the Daulton Gallery in Santa Fe."

She saw him stiffen. "As you said earlier."

"Yes, I wasn't sure you had heard me since you so rudely stomped away as I was mid-sentence."

Amusement briefly fluttered over his face at her boldness and his lips tilted into a slight smirk before he replaced it with his usual frown.

"I am here because I wish to feature your work at the gallery in an exhibition showcase."

"Not going to happen."

"I think, if you heard what I have to say, you might change your mind."

"Doubtful."

"I have sketches of potential displays."

"Good for you."

Flustered with his snippy interruptions, she continued, her temper rising further.

"I have notes on the evening's itinerary."

"Not interested."

"Oh, would you just stop it!" Her voice raised, and she quickly tampered it down with a calming breath and tried to maintain her professionalism.

His brow rose at her outburst and he crossed his arms. *Strong, toned arms,* she noted, and then shook her head of such a thought. *How dare she find anything remotely attractive about the man.* "I think, Mr. Walsh, if you took the time to look over my ideas for your work you would find them quite... pleasing," She finished.

He shook his head slowly. "Again, I am not interested."

"But you have such talent." Her tone turned to exasperated pleading. "And you obviously have pieces just sitting around waiting for buyers. I could help with that."

"I don't want your help."

"But-"

"No buts," he interrupted. "Now, leave." He turned back to his refrigerator and reached inside, shutting her out along with their conversation. Caroline reached into her bag and pulled out her packet of information and tossed it on the table along with her business card. "If you change your mind," she said, as she turned and walked out the way she came.

∞

Finn watched Caroline stalk back to Rory's car, his sister waiting patiently with a welcoming smile and a laugh as he heard Caroline spewing insults at his "pig-headedness." He grinned at that, watching as her heel caught in the grass and almost sent her tumbling. She reached down and slipped her feet out of her shoes and continued her uneven fit back to the car. He chuckled under his breath as she turned to face his house with one last look of disdain before slipping into his sister's car.

The woman had fire and he found he liked that about her. As neat and tidy as her appearance was, her tongue sparked when she grew upset. He watched as she continued ranting to his sister as they hashed out what had just transpired. He knew Caroline would be mortified if she realized he could hear every word she said.

"What a boar of a man," she continued. "I cannot fathom how you two are related." She turned to Rory in complete shock.

Rory laughed. "Sometimes, neither can I."

Caroline blew a frustrated breath and crossed her arms over her middle. "I am sorry, Rory, I am behaving completely unprofessionally, not only speaking this way about your client, but also your brother."

"Don't apologize. I get it." She grinned as she motioned towards the house. "Finn's always been a pain in the rear. Believe it or not, it's one of his most endearing qualities."

"Now I know you're lying. How can being vile be endearing?" Bewildered, Caroline shook her head. "Arghhh," she groaned in frustration. "My blood is still bubbling!" She threw her hands up before resting an arm on the door and looking out the window.

Finn ducked back behind the wall so as not to be seen eavesdropping and waited. He spotted the paperwork and his lips tipped into a slow smile. Why he enjoyed infuriating this particular woman, he didn't know, but the idea of pushing her further seemed more appealing to him than standing in the shadows. He reached for her card and stack of papers and bolstered out the front door towards the car. Caroline stiffened in her seat as she saw him coming towards them.

"Should I drive off?" Rory laughed as Caroline turned to her in confusion.

He slipped the papers through the open window and watched as they plopped into Caroline's lap. "You forgot these."

Caroline fumbled over the papers and stuffed them back out the window into his hands, her green eyes flaming. "No, I did not. Good day, Mr. Walsh."

She nodded towards Rory as Rory cranked the engine. Finn urged the papers back towards the window again and Caroline's anger forced him to take a small step in retreat as a laugh bubbled out of his chest and had Rory turning in surprise. "This is funny to you?" Caroline challenged. She unbuckled her seat belt and threw open the door to stand toe to toe with Finn. Though she only reached him mid chest, she stood her ground. "I have never been so insulted or shocked by such disregard. You, Mr. Walsh, are an utter disappointment." She could tell that arrow hit home because his face darkened at that. She took it further, hoping to drive her point home. "How such ugliness can create such beauty is beyond me."

"You think I'm ugly?" He stepped towards her and her back pressed against the door of the car. Awkwardly caught between him and the car, Caroline stiffened and Finn's steel gaze penetrated her bravado and she groped for the door handle behind her. He placed a firm hand on the top of the door to prevent her from opening it as she fumbled for a response. "Not ugly, physically," she tried to amend, "but inwardly, or... and..." her words trailed off as a full blush worked its way over her face. "I mean, not that you're attractive, just that you're not ugly. And I am..." she caught the small spark in his eyes as he raised the papers up between them. "Surprised," she continued rambling, "that your breathtaking art comes from such," he waited until her hands clasped the papers before pushing off the door and turning to walk away. Her last word, "monstrosity," held no feeling as he left her breathless and reeling. And though he hated the thought of a stranger coming to his home and touching his art, Finn knew he had not seen the last of Caroline Pritchard and that thought, surprisingly, did not aggravate him.

∞

The ride from Finn Walsh's home back to Santa Fe was too long of a drive not to converse with Rory about what all had just happened. For one, Caroline needed Rory on her side to help her coerce Finn into doing a show with the gallery. Despite his distasteful personality, Caroline still wanted his art for the gallery. She considered it an even more challenging task, and she thrived on a challenge.

"I apologize, Rory, for what just transpired. I did not mean to speak ill of your brother or yell at him."

Rory laughed warmly. "No worries. I think yelling at him while calling him attractive isn't necessarily a bad thing."

Embarrassed, Caroline covered her face with her hands. "I'm not good at confrontation."

"Obviously not," Rory added on a chuckle. "I think he found it amusing."

"That wasn't the point."

"I know," Rory continued, "but it intrigued him. I could tell."

"Really?" Caroline asked.

"Yeah." Rory shrugged. "Finn would not have come back out of the house if he weren't somewhat impressed with you. He could have stayed inside and ignored you. But he didn't."

"So I should take it as a positive sign he gave me back my papers?" Sarcasm dripped from her words as she tossed the dreaded papers up onto the dash.

Rory's contagious laugh had Caroline's frown drifting into an annoyed smile. "He is deplorable."

"That he is," Rory stated proudly. "Now you see why I am his spokesperson."

"Clearly."

"But hey, to your credit, you got him to speak more than two words without a door being slammed in your face, and that right there is a huge improvement over the last guy."

"Someone else has tried to commission him in the past?"

"Yep. Ended up completely weird though. The guy would just not give it up and turned more stalker than anything. It took Finn tossing him, literally tossing him out of his shop to get the man to go away."

"He just lifted him up and threw him out?" Caroline asked, the fact her voice held awe more than disapproval eliciting a big grin from Rory.

"Yep. The guy never came around again, and Finn completely stopped conversing with galleries and anyone affiliated with them from that point on. So you can see why he has such a sour taste for-"

"For people like me," Caroline finished.

"Yeah, though I have to say I don't think he wanted to toss you out of his shop."

"Could have fooled me." Caroline ran a hand through her golden hair and sighed.

"Trust me, I know my brother." Rory followed the smooth curves through the mountains with expert ease as they made their way back towards Santa Fe. "So what's your plan now?"

"Not sure yet," Caroline admitted. "But if Finn Walsh thinks he can just toss my ideas back into my face he's got another thing coming."

"Atta girl." Rory beamed. "I'll do whatever I can to help."

"Thanks." Caroline returned her smile.

"To have his work featured on Canyon Road would be incredible. My parents would flip," Rory added. "And Finn, well, he understands it would be a great career move, he genuinely just can't handle people well."

"*No?*" Caroline gasped in mock surprise and had Rory laughing once more.

"I'll try and work on his people skills before the big event."

"You sound confident you can convince him to do it."

"Not me," she corrected. "We."

"What more can I do? Pretty sure he hates me now. I almost broke two of his pieces and I called him ugly."

"On the inside," Rory amended in a nervous voice imitating Caroline's stuttered response from earlier.

Caroline swatted her arm in embarrassment. "I will never live that down, will I?"

"Nope." Rory giggled as she turned the wheel and led them down Canyon Road back towards the gallery.

"Well, whatever I can do, let me know. I'm determined to showcase him at the Daulton."

"Good. Determination is one attribute needed when dealing with my brother." Rory pulled to the curb and Caroline shuffled out the car door. "I'll be in touch, Caroline. Don't give up." She winked as she pulled away and made her way down the street.

Caroline shouldered her bag and turned to survey the gallery front. The afternoon sun bounced off the front windows and she could envision Finn's glass sparkling in its rays. She would not give up. As infuriating a man as he was, he was a brilliant artist. And finding brilliant artists was her job. A job she loved. If sucking up her own pride and approaching Finn Walsh on her own was required, she would do it. *But first*, she thought, *she needed cake.*

«CHAPTER FOUR»

The only reason Finn ever traveled to Santa Fe from his secluded home was to visit Rory or to shop at the Farmer's Market on Saturdays. He tried to time his visit close to lunch time so as to shop quickly, have his usual lunch visit at Dan and Rory's house and then be on his way back to his own house before dark. The market was always crowded. The Railyard was known specifically for the numerous farmers set up in pavilions selling fresh produce and vegetables. And though he hated crowds, Finn considered it a personal quest to force himself to partake in humanity at least once every couple of weeks so as not to completely lose his mind. A child darted past him and bumped his tote bag. The kid turned to apologize but ran off in fear at the restrained anger that was clearly etched on

Finn's face. Why was the kid not walking? It was crowded. Manners dictated walking, not running through all the people. He felt his chest tighten as he smelled the perfume of the elderly woman in front of him. Sickening. With the heat and that smell, he felt suffocated. He pulled at the collar of his t-shirt and inhaled several deep breaths before he lost his nerve and temper and begin storming through the crowd back to his car. He reached a pavilion offering watermelons and he stood as far from the seller and other buyers as he could muster. He turned a melon in his hands and tapped his finger against it.

"That's a nice one."

He looked up to find Caroline Pritchard standing next to him. She smiled. "Nice to see you again, Mr. Walsh."

"It's Finn." He set the melon down and acted as if he were going to walk away. She restrained him with a light touch of her hand on his arm. "Don't rush on my account." She pointed to the melon. "I just saw you and thought I would say hello and see if you've given my offer any more consideration."

"I haven't." His curt answer did not sway her as she grabbed for her own small melon and began fishing in her purse for cash.

Growling, Finn took the melon from her hand and set it back on the stand, the seller slightly annoyed at his interference with a sale. Surprise had her looking up at him.

"You don't want that one," he said shortly and picked up the one he'd previously looked at and handed it to her.

"Oh, thanks." She took it and handed her cash to the seller before looking the melon over. "Why this one?" she asked curiously.

"If you don't know how to choose a melon then why are you buying one?" His question held irritation as he studied her.

A flush lightly stained her cheeks as she slipped the melon into her own tote bag. "Honestly?" she asked.

"It *is* the best policy," he muttered.

"I saw you over here and needed an excuse to come talk to you."

The slight rise to his brow had her nervously glancing around to the other tents. "And I like watermelon, so two birds with one stone, so to speak."

"I see. Well, goodbye." He began walking away.

Caroline gawked at his departing back, but Finn needed air. He did not wish to converse with the pretty gallery manager any longer than necessary. He didn't want to converse with *anyone* else for that matter, and turned his footsteps towards the parking garage where he'd left his vehicle. *Forget Rory and Dan's for today,* he thought.

"Mr. Walsh!" He heard her calling him and kept walking. Perhaps the woman would get the hint he didn't want to speak with her. "Mr. Walsh! Finn!" she yelled once more before her small hand slid under his arm and gripped his elbow. He turned swiftly, catching her off guard and she took two solid steps back. "Do not touch me," he rumbled. His eyes were fierce and had Caroline shrinking further away. "I'm sorry, I didn't mean to-"

"Just take a hint and leave me alone. If I wanted to see or talk to you I would have made the effort."

His words lashed like a slap to the face. She'd never been told so blatantly to leave someone alone. She watched him as his eyes darted about the crowded railyard and saw him cringe as a man shouldered passed him and brushed shoulder to shoulder with him. Panic began filtering into his gaze as his breathing grew heavy. "I have to go."

Worry creased Caroline's brow as she took a step forward. He firmly held up his hand. "Do not follow me," he barked. He noticed the wounded expression on her face and inwardly kicked himself for making someone feel as she did now. But he needed out before he completely lost his mind. He'd been in the railyard too long. He needed to leave, get home, and be alone for a while to straighten out his nerves.

"I am sorry to cause you distress." Her voice was quiet as she stepped further away from him and watched as he turned to leave.

He reached his truck in record time and hurriedly unlocked the doors and slid inside. He gripped the steering wheel. He felt his chest tighten and a numbness begin to work its way from his chest, down his arms, and into his fingers. His vision began to tunnel and he leaned his head back against the headrest and closed his eyes. He tried to steady his breathing, but the anxiety was too strong. His emotions too out of whack. And though he tried to open his eyes and focus on the wall in front of him, all he saw were blotches of light that slowly faded into darkness.

∞

Caroline shouldered her tote and pressed the unlock button on her key fob, the lights of her car flickering in the shaded garage. She opened her trunk and slid the bag inside before walking to her own door. As she reached for her handle she spotted a figure in the truck parked next to her passenger side. Finn. His head hung at an awkward angle and she questioned whether or not to approach him. Fear kept her frozen a full minute until she realized he wasn't moving at all. Panic fueled her footsteps as she hurried towards his truck window. She knocked on the glass but he didn't move. She tried the door handle and surprisingly, it opened. "Finn!" She nudged his shoulder and his head lolled to the side before causing his body to fall towards the steering wheel. "Finn!" She screamed, desperation evident in her voice as she tried to prevent his head from hitting the wheel. She pushed against his chest to hold him against the seat. She tapped his cheek and his lashes fluttered, but he did not waken. She checked his pulse and it beat at a normal rhythm. She reached in her back pocket for her cell phone and searched for Rory's number. Dialing, she prayed his sister answered.

"This is Rory," she greeted warmly.

"Rory, it's Caroline Pritchard."

"Caroline, everything okay?" she asked, noting the obvious panic in her new acquaintance's voice.

"No. It's Finn. He's unconscious!" Her voice rose along with her pulse.

"Where are you?!" Rory's voice became serious as Caroline heard her leaving wherever she was, the slamming of a car door and engine filtering through the line.

"The Railyard, at the Farmer's Market. I bumped into him earlier and he," Caroline bit back a sob as her hand slipped and Finn continued to slide forward. She hoisted herself onto the edge of his seat and allowed his head to rest on her shoulder rather than the steering wheel.

"Where are you now?" Rory's voice repeated.

"Parking garage by Sambusco Center. Do I need to call the ambulance? I should call the ambulance. I should have called them first. Oh my goodness," her voice cracked and Rory yelled into the phone.

"No, do not call the ambulance. He will be fine. He's probably just had an anxiety attack. It happens, especially when he's in a crowd."

"A what?" Caroline brushed her hair out of her eyes and she tried to find a comfortable position under Finn's weighted upper body.

"I'm almost there. Turning in now. What floor?"

"Two." Caroline heard the squeal of tires as Rory pulled up and climbed out of her car followed by a lanky man Caroline assumed was her husband.

Caroline felt the first tear of relief fall down her cheek as Rory darted towards her. "I'm so sorry, I didn't know what to do. He was just... just slumped here."

"You did fine." Rory squeezed her hand before grabbing Finn's face. "Finn," she lightly tapped his cheeks. "Come on big brother, open your eyes."

His lashes fluttered, but his eyes remained closed.

"How long do these attacks normally last?" Caroline asked, rubbing a hand over her cheek in a futile attempt to stop her tears, her body trying to find some way to deal with the stress and worry. She still held most of Finn's dead weight against her as Rory continued tapping his face.

Finally his lashes fluttered and his eyes slowly focused on his sister's face. Confusion clouded his eyes as he turned from her to the upset face of Caroline. He pulled back from her, realizing his head lay against her. He brought his hands to his temples and shook his head. "What happened?"

"Your anxiety got the best of you again. Thought you said you could handle the market today?" Rory admonished, her fear and worry masked by aggravation.

"It was my fault," Caroline chimed in. "I am so sorry." She reached forward to squeeze his hand but stopped herself and ended with an awkward pat before retrieving her hand. "I cornered you."

She could see the slow burn of embarrassment rise up his neck as he realized she had witnessed the extent of his social anxiety. "I'm fine," he snarled as he shot a venomous look in Rory's direction. "I'm going home."

Rory and Dan stepped closer then, Caroline still seated on the edge of Finn's seat, trapped between the three of them.

"You aren't driving anywhere," Dan commanded, "not for a couple of hours at least."

"I'm fine."

"No," Rory added. "No telling how long you've been out. This isn't like you, Finn. Normally you black out and wake up within a few seconds. This was several minutes. You're coming home with us."

"No."

"Stop being stupid, now come on." Rory stepped back to give him room and it was then Finn noticed Caroline's position on his seat.

She jolted when his blue eyes landed on hers. "What are you doing in my truck? Did you follow me? Even after I told you not to?"

Caroline began to slide off the seat but he placed a restraining hand on her wrist. Her pulse jumped and she could tell he felt it as his brows lifted. "I did not follow you." She jerked her hand free and stepped out of his vehicle. "I am parked beside you. Randomly. Completely random parking position. I saw you, and... was scared you were... dead... or something," she finished.

"Thanks for calling me, Caroline. Sorry about this." Rory patted a consoling hand on her shoulder.

Caroline straightened her shirt and offered a forced smile. "No problem. I will just head home now." She turned towards the truck. "I'm glad you are okay, Mister Wa— Finn," she corrected. "I'm glad you are okay, Finn."

She nodded her goodbye and walked around the back of her car to slide into the driver's seat. With a small wave of farewell, she backed out and exited the parking garage on a long exhale loaded with relief.

∞

He felt like a fool. It wasn't like he had anxiety attacks every time he was forced to be around a crowd of people. It just seemed to happen around Caroline. He liked his solitude, she knew that. Unfortunately, she now knew the depth of that desire. He could not handle people. He wasn't completely overcome by anxiety each time he went to the Railyard Market, but being confronted amongst a crowd of people, standing in the middle of the walkway, forcing people to navigate around him, their eyes focusing on him as they passed by was simply too much. Just thinking about the situation had him taking deep breaths as his pulse quickened again. There was a reason he did not speak to people while out and about. There was a reason he executed his tasks quickly and hurried his way home.

The weekend was brutal. Rory and Dan had kidnapped him for more than their two hour requirement, and he'd stared at house plan after house plan as Dan explained which additions they most wanted to add to the house. Not that Finn wasn't excited for them, he was. He just wasn't in the mood. Not when he'd just humiliated himself in front of Caroline Pritchard the day before. Her look of pity that transformed to fear— fear of him— still left a bitter taste in his mouth. He didn't mean to come across as a jerk all the time. He just didn't want someone poking around his life. But he also knew his limits. Rory was right. This particular episode really sent his body in a whirlwind, and if it weren't for Caroline, who knows how long he would have sat in his enclosed vehicle. So he signed the card and tossed the pen back to his sister.

"I'll get right on this." She slipped the small card in her blouse pocket. "Now, can we discuss what Caroline is offering at the gallery?"

"Now, more than ever, I do not want to do it," Finn replied.

"Finn, look, I know you're embarrassed about yesterday, but it's not a big deal."

"I'm not embarrassed."

"Clearly you are." She pointed to his red face.

"This is anger."

Rory laughed at his denial. "Right. Well, push it aside. Because I think you would be missing out on something great if you choose not to do this showcase."

"It's just like any other gallery show, Rory. I won't be missing out on anything different than I have in the past."

"Are you sure about that?" she asked.

Finn didn't like her prying tone. "As far as Caroline Pritchard is concerned, she is just a gallery manager. Nothing more. So yes, I'm sure that I would not be missing out on anything in particular by not displaying my glass in her gallery."

"Who said anything about Caroline?" Rory asked, tilting her head in study of him.

He mumbled under his breath at his assumption and Rory roared in laughter at his discomfort. "So this *is* about Caroline and you just don't want to admit it."

Finn stood from the table and walked towards the living room. He sat in his favorite spot on the couch and reached for the television remote. Rory snatched it from his hand. His eyes narrowed and she could tell his temper was rising, but she grinned any way. "Best leave me alone, Rory. I'm not in the mood."

"Okay. I guess I'll leave then. I'll take this card to the florist and then walk over to the Daulton and tell Caroline you agreed to the showcase."

His jaw dropped. "What?! No. No you will not."

"I'm making a judgment call here, Finn. We need this."

"Again with the 'we.' I saw the house plans, you guys should be fine to start work on that right now. You don't need more commissions to help with that."

"It's not just about the house, Finn." Rory's voice grew in agitation as she reached for her purse, her hand shaky as Finn scrutinized her every movement.

"What do you mean?"

"I mean, we have other plans for certain pieces of our finances."

"Why so cryptic? Why can't you just tell me?"

"Because you wouldn't understand."

"Try me."

"No."

He shifted to the edge of the couch and reached for her hand and she pulled it away. "No, Finn. Sometimes I don't want to tell you everything either. It's between Dan and me."

"You two okay? Marriage wise?"

His genuine concern had her face softening as she nodded. "Yes, it's nothing like that. We love each other deeply."

"Then what is it, Ro? Just tell me. How can I be here for you through thick and thin if you don't let me in?"

"Perhaps you should flip those words back on yourself."

"Maybe another day I will, but for now, we are talking about you." He patted the seat cushion next to him and draped his arm over her shoulders as she sat and leaned into him. "Talk to me, Rory."

On a heavy sigh, she gave in. "We want a baby," she said quietly.

"A baby?" Surprise carried through his tone, but he tried to keep it light. "You guys are wanting to have a baby and that's why you want to add onto the house? Now it makes sense."

"Not *have* a baby, Finn. We *want* a baby. We found out a year ago that Dan cannot have children biologically, so we are wanting to adopt."

Shock washed over him as he studied his little sister and the defeat in her shoulders, the weight of their struggle evident. How had he not noticed?

"I have been so blind," he said.

She patted his leg in reassurance. "Yes, you have."

They both laughed at her brutal honesty and he pulled her into a tighter hug. "You want a baby, Ro?"

She nodded, swiping a hand over her cheek to clear the tears that had silently begun to fall.

"Then let's get you a baby. Tell Caroline the showcase is a go."

Astonished, Rory pulled away from him. "You're serious?"

"Yes." He stood and waited for her to rise to her feet as well. "Now go. Tell Caroline the news. I'm sure she will be pleased. Just don't let her think she had anything to do with my decision. This one is all you, Rory. It is all for you and Dan."

Beaming, Rory jumped into his arms and placed a big, wet smooch on his cheek, squeezing him until he protested. In glee, she bounced towards the door. "Thank you, Finn. I promise this art exhibition will not just be for me. I feel something great is on the horizon for you as well."

He waved her away as he fought back the sentiment and turned towards his kitchen. He heard her footsteps clear the decking and the start of her car. A baby. His baby sister wanted a baby of her own. He shook his head, bewildered by the idea of someone wanting another person in their life. And not just a person, but a tiny person that needed so much time and patience. His sister would be good at that. After all, he'd tested her patience for years, and she had the gumption to deal with whatever he or life tossed her way. Smiling to himself, he pulled a beer from the fridge and popped the top with a satisfying tug. Taking that first smooth sip, he felt the need to be around his glass. With the previous day's happenings and the conversation he just had with Rory, Finn needed to pour himself into his work and relax.

«CHAPTER FIVE»

"Delivery for Ms. Caroline Pritchard." Rory waltzed through the gallery as if she'd frequented the place on a regular basis and headed straight for Caroline's office. Caroline glanced up at her entry and smiled. "Hey, you were on my list to call today."

"No need. I am here." Rory grinned as she slid the flowers and the beautiful vase onto Caroline's desk. "And I come bearing gifts."

"Wow, flowers? To what do I owe the honor?" Caroline reached for the small card.

"They aren't from me," Rory admitted and waited as she saw Caroline's gaze wash over her brother's chicken scratch handwriting.

"Finn?" Caroline asked. She reread the brief note. *'Thanks for helping. F.W.'*

"That's him trying to be thankful," Rory pointed out with obvious pleasure.

"You did not have to do this."

"It wasn't me." She pointed to the card. "It was all him. I just offered to be the messenger."

Not knowing what to do with that tidbit of information, Caroline slid the card back into its small envelope. "How's he feeling?"

Rory waved a hand as she sat. "He's completely fine, more embarrassed than anything."

Understanding washed over Caroline's face. "He has nothing to be embarrassed about. If I had known, I would not have pursued him yesterday at the market." In truth, her heart ached at the thought of her being the cause of such an attack and she suddenly felt she should have been the one to send a bouquet of flowers.

"Well, at least you now have a grasp on why he prefers to be a hermit." Rory pointed out. "Though his attitude still has no excuse."

Caroline smirked at that and shifted some papers on her desk out of the way. "So what brings you by besides the flowers?"

"He's agreed to do the art exhibition showcase."

Stunned, Caroline's jaw dropped as she stared at Rory. Laughing, Rory reached over and nudged it closed with her finger. "How did you manage that?"

"We. We're in this together, remember?"

"Okay, well how did *we* manage that?"

Rory shrugged. "Between the two of us the poor guy didn't stand a chance."

"I have a feeling this is more your doing, but I'll take the win where I can get it." Caroline grabbed a notepad. "So did he give any specific dates he'd prefer?"

"No, but I'm sure we can decide and just let him know when he needs to have pieces ready."

"Okay, well how about two months from now? That would put him showcasing in August, and will hopefully give him time to prepare some statement pieces he may want to display."

"Trust me, he has an entire cabinet full. You should go check them out and see which ones you'd like to use."

"I'm not sure I'm brave enough to venture into his workshop again," Caroline admitted.

"He owes you one."

"No, he doesn't. At least, I don't want him to feel indebted to me. I honestly did nothing. I just made a phone call. And that would not have even been necessary if I had just left him alone." Still annoyed with how she handled the situation, Caroline leaned back in her chair and squeezed the bridge of her nose.

"He's on board for the show, Caroline. He'll tolerate your presence around his shop to pick out pieces. And if he does get all grouchy about it, then you remind him that this exhibit is for me."

Caroline waited a beat, pondering what Rory meant by that, but nodded reluctantly. "Okay, I'll do it. I will try to swing by there tomorrow morning and talk out the details with him."

"I do have one catch though," Rory held up a finger as her sandaled foot bounced over her crossed legs. "He will not make an artist appearance at the showing. I will be there to field any interest or questions from patrons, but I'm sure you can now understand why Finn cannot be there."

And as disappointed as Caroline was that Finn would not witness his art being appreciated or see it shine across the gallery, she completely understood his desire not to come. "I do understand."

"I knew you would. I know sometimes his gruff remarks seem like personal attacks, but in reality he just doesn't like people to know his struggle."

"And I understand that too. I won't push him on this choice. We can make the evening a success with or without him there."

"Then we have a deal." Rory reached across the table and shook her hand. "We can talk numbers when you begin drafting the contract."

Caroline nodded. "Sounds good. Thanks for stopping by Rory. And thanks— well, tell Finn thanks for the flowers."

Rory winked before shouldering her purse. "You betcha. Oh," she snapped her fingers. "I forgot. Dan and I are having a small barbeque this next weekend. We'd love for you to come."

Flattered but unsure as to whether or not she should mix business with pleasure, Caroline hesitated.

"Come on now, Caroline," Rory coaxed. "It will be fun."

"You sure you don't want to see the contract first?" She teased.

"No. Art show or no art show, I've determined we will be friends. It's not a large gathering, just a few close friends and my parents. And Finn will be there as well, so you will at least have someone you know to talk to."

"Because he just loves talking to me." Caroline waved away her comment. "Okay, I'll come."

"Great, I'll text you the details."

Caroline watched Rory dart out the door and heard her footfalls through the main exhibit hall before the swish of the front doors announced her exit. She then dropped her pen and bolted to her feet with a shout of glee. Regaining her composure, she grabbed her notepad and walked through the gallery room by room to make additional notes for Finn's show. She couldn't believe he'd agreed to do it. Wondering what changed his mind, she dodged Ed as he buffed the floors and grinned in welcome.

She really could not continue her plans until she saw some example pieces he wished to use. She tapped her pencil to her lips and decided to call and let him know she'd be stopping by the following day but quickly remembered she did not have his phone number. Turning up unannounced again did not appeal to her, but what choice did she have? She walked back to her office and eyed the flowers he'd sent her. It was then that her gaze landed on the vase. It was one of his pieces. She lifted it to marvel at its mixture of green hues and wondered what made him think to give her this one. *He probably did not even pick it out*, she mused. Rory probably grabbed it on her way out of his shop and had the florist use it. Not overthinking it, she set the vase of blooms on her window sill and began a checklist of what she needed to go over with Finn the following day.

∞

He'd spent the entire night working on the piece that had haunted his thoughts since the day at the market, and he'd finished in the wee hours of the morning. Though his eyes felt gritty and his face itched from the new stubble gracing his chin and cheeks, Finn needed to see it. He'd left it in the annealing oven overnight, and he took a deep breath in hopes that it survived without cracking. It had been a while since he'd created such a massive piece, and his muscles still ached from the constant movements required to hoist such a piece by himself for the entire process.

He opened the annealing oven and there it sat. A ray of sun landed on it and refracted through the different layers of glass, sprinkling the most brilliant gemstones across the workshop. He turned at the sound of a gasp and saw Caroline standing in the doorway of his shop, her hand slowly rising to cover her mouth as her wide eyes soaked in the image before her. She walked towards him and gently laid her hand on his arm as her eyes never left the piece. "Finn," was all she whispered as her hand reached to touch but she pulled it back instinctively remembering what happened the last time she'd attempted such a task.

He hadn't wanted anyone to see it yet, but he quickly found himself staring at Caroline's reaction versus the stunning art before him. Her response to his work was all he needed to turn his annoyance at her presence into pride. Though she was breaking his biggest rule, again, by entering his shop, her stunned expression was priceless.

"How did you do this?" she marveled, looking up at him in awe, her green eyes the perfect match to the green silhouette before them. The mix of green glass stood willowy and soft, with seductive curves and smooth textures, while the bright blue piece wove around the green in a shot of vibrant hues of sapphire. "Is it two figures?"

"What do you think it is?" he asked, curious to see if she interpreted his art the way he did.

"Oh," she paused to study the piece further, her hand rising to touch again and yet restrained by her own fear of Finn's wrath. The action made him grin behind her. The ache to touch and absorb was one of the biggest compliments to an artist. "I feel like this green piece symbolizes a woman and the blue either a dark force or a man... a mad man," she whispered. The bold blue piece sent chills up her arms, but when she stepped back to survey the work in its entirety, the two halves blended, curved, and swayed together to create a stunning masterpiece of glasswork. "I'm just in awe, Finn."

Pleased, he smiled at her back, but when she turned around his expression was neutral. "What do you call it?"

"Beautiful Fury."

She repeated the name and turned to the piece once more. "Yes, it's quite fitting." She turned back to him with a sheepish smile, "I kind of wish I could buy it for myself."

He shrugged as if her statement did not affect him, though he felt a warmth spread in his chest in response to the stars in her eyes as she looked the piece over once more.

"I came by today to talk about the exhibition show. Rory said you agreed to do it."

He reached into the annealing oven and lifted the piece out and she watched as he carried it over to his work bench and sat it down while he fished in his pocket for a key to the dark cabinet against the wall. When he opened the doors, Caroline gasped and pushed passed him, her eyes soaking in all the glass hidden in secret. She swung a hand and hit his shoulder as a laugh bubbled forth from her lips in disbelief at not only her actions but the exquisite pieces he left locked away.

"What was that for?" he asked, rubbing his shoulder.

Without pity, Caroline just shook her head at him. "I cannot believe you hide these away, Finn. Why do you have them locked in a cabinet?"

"Because I don't want to sell them."

"But what purpose do they serve just sitting in here?" she pressed, not noticing the change in his expression until he faced her.

"My business is my own," he barked.

She watched as he carefully transferred 'Beautiful Fury' into the cabinet. He reached to close the doors but she grabbed his hand. "Wait." She stepped towards the piece and ran a fingertip down the long stroke of blue glass. "I can't believe you're locking this away." Her whisper and imploring gaze drew him closer towards her, his hand still holding the door but braced above her head. She backed up as he cornered her against the exposed shelves. Caroline's pulse skyrocketed as she watched his eyes narrow as they searched her face. "Move."

The command had her stiffening and defiance crossed her face as she fisted her hands on her hips. "You're such a—"

"Such a what?" he asked, nudging her aside as he closed the doors and clipped the lock in place.

"Scrooge," she finished.

"My work, my rules." He slipped the key into his pocket and began walking out of the shop forcing her to follow him.

"Well are you willing to part with any of the pieces in your shop? I mean, if we are to showcase your art we actually *need* your art."

He ignored her as he made his way towards his house and she kept incessantly talking and asking questions.

"I need to know what pieces you want to use so I can modify my layout of the gallery. I want to make sure they are displayed in the best manner, and to do that, I need to know what I am to be using."

He opened the door and walked inside, this time, to her relief, he did not shut her out but expected her to follow him. And she did. "And I still can't fathom why you have those gorgeous sculptures just sitting in a cabinet in a dusty work shop. Who *does* that?" Her hands moved briskly as she spoke and she followed him down a narrow hallway. He turned then and she bounced right off his chest with a small grunt.

"Must you follow me everywhere?"

"I'm just trying to understand you, Finn."

"Well, how about you ponder Finn Walsh out there." He pointed towards the other end of the hallway that led to his living room.

"But—"

He threw a hand over her mouth before she could start into her exasperating rant once more. "I'm going to use the restroom, Caroline. If you really must follow me, I'd appreciate it if you closed your eyes."

Horrified with herself and his abruptness, Caroline stepped back. "I apologize. I didn't realize—"

As she fumbled for something to say, he slowly turned her shoulders and nudged her the opposite direction. When he saw her walking towards the living room, he slipped inside his bedroom for a quick breather. He hadn't meant for her to see 'Beautiful Fury.' Not yet any way. But her reaction to the piece made him smile. He waited a moment more until his frustration slowly ebbed away and then walked back out into the living area. She perched, straight-backed and full of nervous energy on the edge of his couch. She hopped to her feet when he entered and immediately began following him as he made his way to his kitchen.

"So I have a list of things I'd like to go over with you about the exhibit."

"I'm sure you do." He reached into the fridge and grabbed a bottle of water. Without offering her one, he walked towards the sliding glass door that led to his deck, Caroline hot on his heels. The woman was insufferable. Her determination, though somewhat amusing, was borderline obsessive.

He sat and waited for her to sit as well. Instead of sitting across from him, she sat in the chair next to him. He tensed at the close proximity, but waited for her to finish explaining why she came to his house.

"I made a list for you so that I do not have to explain everything and watch you purposely ignore it." She handed him a stapled packet. "This is also the contract. I've already talked the details out with Rory and she said there shouldn't be a problem there. So, I just need you to sign it." He skimmed over the page, flipped to the next one and set his beer down.

"Thirty percent?"

"Hmmm?" She looked up from her other notes. "Oh, yes, that's the percentage the gallery will receive from your total sales."

"I don't think so."

"Why not? Rory found it quite reasonable."

"I'm sure she did. But I do not. Ten percent."

"*Ten*?" She laughed at the absurdity. "I don't think so."

"Well, I'm not giving you a single piece of glass until you change this from thirty percent."

"How about twenty percent?"

"Fifteen. Nothing more than that. I want Rory to get as much as possible," he countered.

"Done." She did not wish to haggle with him further and stopped the negotiation there before they were both upset. "Wait, Rory?"

She saw the regret flash across his face before he covered it with a scowl. "I want to make enough that she receives a good cut as well."

"She will. We all will. Even at thirty percent," Caroline replied.

"We just agreed to fifteen." He pointed at her and she rolled her eyes as she reached for the contract, penned over the thirty with a fifteen and initialed next to it. She held the pen out to him.

"Now will you sign?"

"I need to finish reading it." He picked up the stack of papers again and she sighed as she leaned back in her chair and surveyed her surroundings.

After a long pause, she turned towards him. "You really do have a nice spot up here."

Finn growled as he tossed the papers and pen onto the table. "Can you not be quiet for more than two seconds?"

"I was just complimenting your home."

"And I'm reading." He pointed to the papers.

Huffing in irritation, she turned her attention back to the scenery around her and allowed him to continue reading.

"This was your family home, right?"

Groaning, he fisted his hands on his lap as he looked at her. The sun casting rays through the trees had her blonde hair shining, the fine strands gently fluffed from the light breeze. He stared several long moments before he saw her fidget in her seat. She remained quiet as he turned back to the papers and finished reading. He grabbed the pen and signed his name.

A relieved smile washed over her face as she reached for the papers before he could change his mind. "Alright, so now—"

"We're done. You can leave." He tried to stand but she plopped a hand over his arm again, and he didn't like the spark that popped between them. She jumped at the contact. "You shocked me." She accused, as she shook relief into her hand.

"Shouldn't have touched me then."

"Fine." She slid the contract into her bag and stood at the same time he did. "I left the other information on your coffee table, so you can look it over. We have a couple of months, so I don't want you to feel I'm rushing you. But once you have some pieces you're willing to part with, send them my way. I can store them in the gallery until the exhibit."

He nodded curtly that he understood.

"Also," she took a step closer and he took a step back. "I would like to use 'Beautiful Fury' as the focal piece in the main hall."

"No."

"Finn," she began to plead, and he shook his head.

"You weren't even supposed to see that."

Sighing, she ventured one last request. "Just think about it, please."

He shoved his hands into his pant pockets as she began making her way towards her car. Turning on the steps she studied him a moment. "By the way, thank you for the flowers… and the vase."

"What vase?"

"The one the flowers came in. It was one of yours. I assumed you picked it out. My mistake."

Surprised by her displeasure, he amended his reply. "Oh, right. Um, no problem."

Her eyes lifted to his and held a moment before a small smile tilted her lips. "See you around, Finn."

He watched as she slid into her car and offered a small wave before pulling out and heading back towards Santa Fe. He reached into his pocket and pulled out his phone and dialed his sister.

"Hey, big brother," she greeted.

"Don't ever agree to thirty percent again, and don't ever steal from my shelves to give a vase away without asking first." He hung up and stormed his way back into the house.

«CHAPTER SIX»

It was a perfect day. The sun was shining and the gallery was bright and welcoming, the broad glass windows in the front of the building bringing sunshine inside to warm the space and lighten the mood of all who entered. Caroline spent most of her morning walking throughout the rooms and interacting with patrons. The part of the job most people did not care for, she actually loved.

The empty nesters from east Texas who decided to spend their vacation split between Santa Fe and Taos, expressed excitement over the local artists featured throughout the gallery, particularly the pottery.

The elderly couple from Tennessee, somewhere between their seventies and eighties, were taking a second honeymoon, as they called it. They purchased one tapestry for their daughter's Arizona home because "it matched."

Caroline loved them all. All the stories, the lives full of different experiences and backgrounds. She loved meeting them, even for the briefest of moments. She loved people. All shapes, sizes, colors, personal histories... she just loved people. So she could not help feeling frustrated that her mind continued to wander to the one person she did not care for: Finnegan Walsh.

Okay, so she had started to appreciate the man behind the art, just a smidgen. Not for his kindness, because the man possessed hardly any. But for the vulnerability he tried to hide, the pride in his work, the tenderness with which he treated his sister and her husband. These were the small attributes that had slowly begun to impress Caroline. As hard of a man as Finn was, she could not deny he had a certain *je ne sais quoi* that caused her to think of him throughout the day for various reasons. Frowning at her reflection in a refracted glass urn, she inwardly scolded herself for thinking of him yet again.

She heard her office phone ringing and made her way there. "Daulton Gallery," she greeted.

"Hey, it's Rory."

"Hey!" Caroline reached to close her office door. "How's it going?"

"Pretty peachy. What are you doing for lunch today?"

"Probably Frank's, why? Care to join me?"

"I would love to." The smile in Rory's tone had Caroline grinning.

"Eleven-thirty?"

"Yes! Because I am starving!"

"See you in a few minutes." Caroline hung up the phone and sent the line to voicemail and stepped out the door and locked it.

"Off again, Ms. Caroline?" Ed asked, his polishing rag tossed carelessly over his shoulder as he pulled on a new set of latex gloves.

"Headed to lunch, Ed. I should be back in an hour or so."

"Yes ma'am." He tapped the bill of his cap in response as he continued on his way down the hall.

Stepping outside, Caroline turned out the door in the direction of Frank's Bistro and slammed right into Finn Walsh. She caught herself from stumbling by gripping his arms. He recoiled quickly as if scalded by her touch until he realized it was her. She saw a smug smile trace over his face.

"Finn." Breathless, she straightened her purse strap. "What are you doing here?"

"I came to look at the gallery."

"But I'm headed out."

"That's fine."

"I'm meeting Rory for lunch," she explained. "You can come with me if you want. And once we're finished up there I can give you a tour of the gallery and discuss my ideas with you."

"No. I'll just take a look around now."

"But I won't be here." She stepped to the side to block his path as he tried to move around her.

"Even better," he replied.

He stepped through the door and Caroline followed. He turned and had her biting back a sharp retort when he held up his hand and blocked her face before she could utter a syllable. "Stop following me and go to lunch, Caroline. I'll take a look around myself. I don't need a guide." He eased away from her, the feel of her frustrated sigh still heating his hand.

"Fine." She straightened her blazer. "If you have any questions just leave a note on my office door."

Without agreeing, Finn continued his slow, measured steps into the gallery. Caroline hovered a moment longer before relinquishing her desire to show off the space and headed to meet Rory.

When she reached Frank's, Rory waved her over to the table. "Come. Sit. Eat. Devour." Rory grinned as she shoved a potato chip into her mouth and crunched.

"Sorry I'm a few minutes late, but your brother showed up at the gallery."

"Finn?"

"Do you have another brother?" Caroline asked.

"Well, no... but by the way he's been acting lately it kind of seems like it." Rory laughed. "What did he want?"

"To tour the gallery. On his own."

"Ah. Good. I'm glad he's making the effort."

"I wish I was there to show him my ideas, but he insisted he did not need me to."

"He'll be fine."

"Yes, but—"

"Caroline," Rory groaned. "You should know by now that Finn would much rather do things alone. If he wanted you to guide him around he would have waited for you, or better yet, scheduled a tour with you. Let him be. If he feels pushed into anything he'll crawl back into his mouse hole and never come out again."

"You're right." Caroline took a deep breath as she held up a finger to Matilda and moved her hands to motion which number on the menu she wanted for lunch so Matilda did not have to make the trip to the table. "He just... gets under my skin." Caroline said, taking a sip of water. "It's like he just knows how to press my buttons and get me all stirred up, and not in a good way."

Suppressing a smile, Rory listened and watched as Caroline glanced at her phone. "Clock watching already? Am I that bad of a date?"

"I'm sorry. No. Well, yes, in regards to clock watching. I'm hoping he is still there when we are finished."

"He won't be."

"Ugh." Caroline dropped her head in her hands and smoothed back her hair as she looked at Rory. "I know."

"Then why worry about it?"

"What if he doesn't like the gallery? What if it's not big enough or new enough? There's plenty of choices on Canyon Road. He could walk into any of them and ask for a showcase."

"You're worrying over nothing. He agreed to Daulton. He agreed to you. He won't walk into another gallery and choose someone else."

Nervously, Caroline drummed her fingers on the table. "You're right. I know you're right. You're his sister. You know him better than anyone."

"That I do," Rory agreed with a wink. "Trust me on this one okay."

Nodding, Caroline slowly began to relax as Matilda delivered her bowl of soup and Rory began talking about the upcoming barbecue scheduled for tomorrow.

"You're still coming, right?"

"Yes."

"Good. It should be fun. Dan and I sort of have an announcement to make and we want everyone there."

Touched to be included in what seemed like an important announcement, Caroline reached forward and squeezed Rory's hand. "I can't wait to hear what it is."

"Thanks." A shyness swept over Rory's face and she covered it by taking a hearty bite of her sandwich. "Finn is going to flip."

Not knowing what the news would be, Caroline was surprised to hear Rory would want to cause Finn to be angry. "Upset?"

"No. He already knows what it is all about, he just doesn't know the latest news."

"Why will he flip?"

"Let's just say things sometimes move faster than we imagine."

"Do you think he needs to be..." Caroline did not know how to phrase her question, but felt Finn's anxiety should not be provoked.

Rory's smile softened at Caroline. "You're worried about him."

"Well, yes, aren't you?"

"Not really." Rory snickered at Caroline's dumbfounded expression. "He can handle himself, Caroline. He doesn't just faint on a whim. He's a tough guy. Don't baby him."

"I'm not babying him," Caroline defended. "I was just... asking." She trailed off as she glanced at her phone once more.

Rory grinned as she slid her credit card into the black binder for Matilda to swing by and pick up. The attraction Caroline held towards Finn was obvious. Not to Caroline, Rory realized, but to everyone else. She wasn't sure if Finn recognized the gallery manager's feelings either, though probably not considering her brother's observation skills were next to nil when it came to people and their emotions. She wasn't even sure anyone could break through Finn's rough exterior to the kind heart beneath. But she had also never met a woman with such determination as Caroline Pritchard. And it was noticeable that Finn too had some sort of feelings towards Caroline, whether simply genuine disregard or romantic interest, Rory could not tell just yet. But her brother tolerated the woman, and that was new altogether.

"Well, that was delicious." Rory jumped to her feet as Caroline accepted her change from Matilda and began sliding it into her wallet. "Thanks for the quick meet up."

"For sure. It's nice to get out of the office every once in a while."

"I bet." Rory flung her purse strap over her head and draped it against her hip, the small cross body bag a Native American weave sewn into leather. *Santa Fe style at its finest*, Caroline thought as she slipped her plain black purse over her shoulder. "I'll see you tomorrow, then."

"See ya." Rory waved as she headed the opposite direction. Caroline forced herself to walk at a normal pace though she prayed Finn was still at the gallery. When she entered, she headed towards her office and disappointment swamped her as she found no notes taped to her door. She unlocked the door and turned on the lights. She gasped as she took a slow step forward and found 'Beautiful Fury' sitting upon her desk with a small note taped to the glass. *"Not for sale. But here's a focal piece for the show. You're welcome. F.W."*

∞

Finn knew Caroline would show up at his front door as soon as she spotted the sculpture on her desk. He still couldn't fathom why he took it to her, or why he agreed to let her use it for the showcase. In fact, he'd been kicking himself the moment he left the Daulton. He saw her little car drive up the dirt lane and tamped down his personal frustrations and attempted to redirect them towards her. She was cute, hopping out of her car with a bounce to her step, pure joy shining on her face as she bounded towards his work shop. That did it. That shifted his mood immediately as he stormed down the deck towards his studio. She didn't even knock, she just walked right inside, completely unaware that he might actually be at his house.

He stepped into the shop and saw her turning to look for him. "No one is allowed in my work shop. How many times must I repeat myself?!" His voice boomed through the silence and she jumped as she turned to face him. Shrinking a tad, she ran a hand through her sandy hair.

"Why don't you put a lock on the door then?"

"Probably because I never had anyone coming to visit before you started nosing your way into my work." He shoved past her, flicked the switch to his furnace, and checked the gas gauges on the side. It would take a while for the temperature to rise, but if he set it now, then he could possibly work out his aggravation in glass as soon as she left.

"I'm going to let that one go, because I am in such a good mood." She ran towards him and stopped, her smile beaming up at him and her green eyes shining. She swung her arms around him, her head resting against his chest as she squeezed him in a tight embrace. He didn't move. Not an inch. Not even to raise a hand for a slight tap on her back in response. He didn't quite know how to respond. Other than Rory, he did not accept hugs from other people. It stressed him out. But something about Caroline's enthusiastic embrace had him scrabbling for what to say and how to act. *He was mad at her, wasn't he? Yes, he was mad at her for entering his work shop.* Sticking with his original plan to be upset, he felt her arms ease their grip and she stepped back. "Thank you for the sculpture."

"It's not yours to keep. I thought the note was clear."

She rolled her eyes at his usual rude tone. "I know that. I meant thank you for letting me use it in the showcase." She waited for him to say something but he just began fluttering about his shop pulling jars of different chemicals, color powders, and tools and laying them out on his work bench.

"It was nice of you," she coaxed, hoping for some response.

He continued working.

"Argh," she stomped her foot and had him glancing her direction.

"Did you say something?"

"Oh please." Caroline stalked towards him but paused in her lecture as she watched him pour colored grit onto the bench. "What's that?" She stuck her hand out to rub her fingers over it and he snatched her wrist. "What is it with you and touching? Keep your hands to yourself. This is a work space for crying out loud."

"Sorry," she whispered. She continued to watch him work and for once she was silent.

He grabbed a color bar and placed it in a large bag and sealed it. He then pounded it with a hammer, shattering the glass into tiny pieces. He then poured it out on the workbench as well. When his station was set, Finn moved to the other end of the table and adjusted the tools he had laid out before moving his chair over. Caroline stood like a statue on the other side of the table. "If you refuse to leave, then you need to wear these." He shoved safety goggles her direction and she hesitantly reached for them as she eyed him closely. "I can stay?"

"Just don't talk. And please, for pity's sake, do not touch anything."

She nodded.

"There's a stool over there. You'll want to sit."

She hurried over to the metal stool and started to lift it but it would barely budge. Instead, she began dragging it across the floor. The sound was as irritating as silverware scraping china and had Finn's frustration brewing. She pulled it to where she'd previously stood and sat. Then stood and pulled it a bit closer, the screeching noise echoing in the room. Sat. Not right, stood, screech, sat. She stood to make another minor adjustment and he tossed a tool on the table. "Would you just *sit* down?!"

She grimaced in apology and held up her hands in peace. "Sorry." She waved her hand for him to continue. "Can you tell me what it is you plan to make?"

"A vase."

"What sort of vase?"

"Does it matter?"

"I was just curious," she shrugged.

"It's a vase to replace the one given to you without my consent," he barked, and saw a brief flash of hurt dart into her eyes. He pinched the bridge of his nose. "Look, I didn't mean that. I just... really need you to be quiet."

She nodded, but he detected her hurt feelings from across the table and for once, actually felt bad for causing them.

"Could you explain to me the process as you make it?"

"Why?"

"I find it fascinating, and I think it would add some depth to my discussions with patrons on the night of your exhibit."

Smart, he thought. And she was probably right that it would give her some interesting feedback on a few of his pieces.

"Alright, here's the deal." He made sure his eyes met hers as he spoke. She hung on every word. "If I walk you through this, you have to stay over there at all times. I tell you what I want to tell you. There's some things that are strictly mine to know."

"Understood." She flashed an excited smile and sat on her hands so as not to risk touching anything, and her eagerness to watch and learn intrigued him.

"Alright..." He grabbed for a tool.

"What is that?"

He dropped his chin to his chest and she began apologizing for speaking. A low rumble bubbled up from his chest as he laughed, catching her by surprise even more. He rubbed a hand over his mouth to try and stop it, but he couldn't help it. "You just can't help yourself, can you?"

A slow grin spread over her face as she sat in awe of seeing him laugh. "I will do my best to listen before talking, Mr. Walsh." She saluted him and he pointed to her hand. She quickly tucked it back under her thigh and nodded that she was ready to begin.

His smile didn't fade. In fact, for most of the beginning stages her questions were surprisingly astute. What gases did he use to reach such high temperatures in the furnace? What chemicals produced what colors? Why did he puff into the blow pipe the way he did? He didn't mind explaining to her, and eventually they fell into a smooth process that surprised them both.

«CHAPTER SEVEN»

He rolled from the glory hole back to the work bench and continued shaping the molten glass. Her eyes burned from staring at the blazing ball on the end of his blow pipe, but she could not turn away. Mesmerized, she leaned forward and watched the bubble expand. Finn took slow, deep puffs and the bubble grew. He'd pause and blow three consecutive spurts of short puffs. Then he'd roll back to the glory hole to reheat the glass. His hands constantly turned the pipe as he worked, and Caroline was amazed with his steady rhythm. He turned towards her, but kept his pipe in the fire as he spoke. "Come to my side of the table."

"I thought you wanted me to stay right here."

"Just move," he ordered.

She did as she was told, unsure of what he was wanting her to help with, but willing.

"Put those gloves on." He nodded towards a spare set of gloves tucked into a basket hanging on the edge of the bench. She slid them on, her slim arms swallowed up by the oversized mitts. He rolled back over and stood. "Now take the pipe." She looked up at him stunned. His hands continued to turn it as he spoke. "Take the pipe, Caroline."

She stepped closer and he continued rotating the pipe with his left hand as he used his other to place her hand in the right position. "See how I'm turning it?"

She nodded.

"Good. Now use your other hand and continue turning the pipe for me." She obeyed, and he stepped to the side as she turned the pipe. "What now?" She looked up at him and he shook his head. "Never take your eyes off the glass." He did not have to tell her twice. He watched her a minute as she tried desperately hard to mimic his movements, but her rotations were choppy and the glass began to droop on one side. He placed his hands over hers and assisted in retraining her rotation. He was close, practically wrapping his arms around her and his heady scent of musk, heat, and outdoors flooded her senses. She laughed, the sound awkward as he shifted to look at her face.

Yes, she was crazy, and no, he had no idea what she was thinking. *Thank the Lord,* she thought, *or he'd run straight to his house and lock himself inside.*

He let go of her hands and then walked towards the glory hole, opening the cover. "Now stick it in the glory hole again, we need to heat it up. Keep turning," he ordered, but his voice did not hold its usual sharpness. Her arms were growing tired and her muscles felt fatigued. She couldn't understand how he did this for hours on end.

"Now come to the table."

She obeyed, and he guided the pipe towards the frit scattered along the bench and rolled the glass through. She watched as the different tiny pieces stuck to the melted glass. "Now back to the glory hole."

"Again?" she asked, the first signs of fatigue showing as she made the short trek once more. He grinned at her back as she expertly opened the cover to the hole and stuck the pipe inside, her rotations never stopping.

"This trip is important," he explained. "This will melt the colored glass into the clear glass." She held it for a couple of minutes and then he tilted his head towards the table. She moved back to the work bench and he lightly placed a hand on her hip to guide her steps to a different position and spot at the edge of the table. "Rest the pipe there, but keep turning it." He grabbed several tools and sat in his chair. He puffed several breaths into the pipe and she watched it expand, the rich purples and blues swirled together, the blend of shades seeping into one another. He then pointed towards the glory hole and she made the trip and back again without guidance. He then began shaping the piece. Pulling here, tugging there, until a small elongated shape begin to take form. He then reached for the punty and stuck it in the furnace to retrieve a small gather and stuck it to the bottom of the piece. "Now for the hard part. No more turning." Her hands froze, and her arms screamed. He rapped the blow pipe and the transfer to the punty was a success. He then handed it back to her and pointed towards the glory hole.

He waved her back to the bench and she watched now as he worked quickly and smoothly to create a mouth to the vase. When he was satisfied, he placed his hand at the small of her back and nudged her towards the opposite end of the bench as she carried the punty and vase. He placed a finger under her elbow and pushed upward until the vase rested several inches above a fire proof blanket in a box. He then tapped the punty and the vase broke away, landing in the blanket. He then took the punty from her hands and rested it back in the fire.

"Is it finished?" Caroline looked up at him and he shook his head.

"Now pick it up." She reached over, the gloves protecting her hands from the heat, and followed him to another chamber. "This is the annealing oven. It will be placed in here, and the temperature slowly decreases over several hours and cools the glass. *Then* it will be finished."

Amazed that she had just created a vase, Caroline lifted her goggles on top her head. "I cannot believe I just did that!" She removed the gloves and placed them back into the metal basket on the bench. Finn walked over to a small refrigerator and grabbed two cans of soda. "You earned it." He popped the top and handed one to her and then did the same for himself.

"Now let's get out of here." He walked out of the shop and waited until she followed then closed the door. They walked in companionable silence up to his deck and sat on the stairs facing the setting sun. The sky as vibrant as some of his glass, Caroline soared on the high of creating something from nothing.

"I can see why you love it," she said, turning to him with a soft smile on her lips. "Thanks for teaching me."

"You," he started, before taking a long sip of his soda. "were a surprisingly good student."

She gaped at him and then laughed. "And why would I not be?"

"I did not think you capable of keeping quiet for so long."

"Oh really?" She took the teasing in stride as he chuckled, his gaze absorbing the colors surrounding them. "I was too tired. The constant turning of the pipe has left me achy. How do you do it?" She glanced at him once more. "Are you creating new designs right now?"

"What do you mean?"

She waved her hand towards the sunset. "Is this good inspiration?"

"Sometimes."

She finished her soda and placed the can on the step in front of her and then stomped on it, the action surprising him. She then noticed his reaction and laughed, a blush of embarrassment staining her cheeks. "Oh, do you not do that?"

He shook his head and watched as she tossed it into the trash can behind them. Shrugging she crossed her arms over her knees. "My dad taught me that when I was little and it sort of stuck." Self-conscious at his open study of her, she patted her legs and stood. "I should go. It's a pretty long drive back."

"Right." Finn stood and walked with her towards her car.

"Thank you again... for delivering the sculpture today." She opened her door, his hand sliding to the top to hold it open as she tossed her purse towards the passenger side. When she turned, he stood closer than anticipated and she froze a moment before continuing. "And for letting me experience your work first hand. It is truly remarkable, Finn." His face was void of emotion, but his eyes burned through her and she felt like she was staring into the glory hole all over again. "I'll see you at Rory's barbecue tomorrow?"

He nodded.

Caroline smiled, disappointed that her great afternoon and evening was coming to an end, but glad that she would have a chance to see him tomorrow. "Well, I'll see you then."

She started to slide into the car, but Finn placed his hand over her shoulder and spun her back around. His lips landed on hers before she could even think, and though his touch was firm, his lips were soft as they glided over hers. She felt his hand move from her shoulder to her cheek. When she leaned closer to him, and her hand moved from the door handle to his arm, he jumped back. Her head reeling and her mind adjusting back to reality, she stood silent and still. Finn's face was a mixture of shock and then slowly, regret, as he spun on his heels and hurried back to his house. Sliding, though somewhat more like melting, into her front seat, Caroline buckled her seat belt and stared at the last remaining traces of sunlight as they disappeared behind the trees. *What just happened?* Forcing her body to move, she traced a finger over her lips, the tingle Finn left behind slowly faded into a warm flutter in her stomach. *What had just happened?* She turned the key and backed out of Finn's driveway and despised the man for tormenting her thoughts on the long drive back to Santa Fe.

∞

Finn slammed the door behind him as he made his way to the shower. He could not believe he'd kissed her. He stepped into the cold spray, punishing himself with its icy temperature for being so stupid. *Why had he done it?* Leaning his head back into the spray, he cringed as the freezing water pounded against him. He reached and turned on the hot water. Enough was enough. He couldn't change what happened. Now he just had to deal with the slip up. And lucky him, he'd see her tomorrow. How fitting. He couldn't just wait a few days and let the moment fizzle out naturally, no, he had to face her at his sister's bloody barbecue!

He shoved off the water and stepped out, toweling off his hair. They'd had a good day in the work shop. His emotions were always out of whack after a successful day. The artist rush. He was on a high. Yeah, that was a good excuse. He wasn't thinking straight. She'd believe that.

His own frown in the mirror did not convince him. Maybe she wouldn't bring it up. Growling, he trudged into his bedroom, grabbed the first available t-shirt and dragged it over his head. It was Caroline, she would blabber about anything. She would most definitely bring it up. He sat on the edge of his bed and thought about the day. He couldn't understand why he even allowed her to touch his work, much less let her create a piece.

Liar, he told himself. He knew exactly why he did it, because he could still see the hurt in her eyes from his comment about the vase Rory had given her. She had wanted it to be from him and had considered it a special gift. That thought intrigued him for one, but the fact she stuck around afterwards to ask questions about the process showed her gumption. He had meant the comment to be hurtful, and it hit true to mark. What he hadn't expected was to feel remorse for hurting her. And what's more, he hadn't expected to feel like he should make her feel better. Any other person, he wouldn't care how she felt. So why Caroline? Why was he sitting in his room contemplating the different shades of green in her eyes and the smell of her hair? The small sway of her lower back as he guided her around the work bench. The radiance of the glass reflecting off her face and the sheer joy she felt at receiving 'Beautiful Fury.'

She appreciated his work. That was always a good feeling, but to kiss her for it? No. Wrong move. Walking towards the kitchen, he plopped a frying pan on the stove top and grabbed an onion and started chopping. His phone rang and his lip snarled. She couldn't even drive home without already wanting to hash it out. He grabbed the receiver. "Caroline, so help me I will hunt you down, snatch you, and throw you off the nearest mountain if you come back here right now." His voice held its usual rudeness, but the subject matter intrigued his caller.

"Well hello to you too, big brother." Rory's amused voice filtered over the line and had him shaming himself under his breath.

"Hey. What do you want?"

"Just wanted to make sure you were still coming tomorrow."

"I said I would."

"I know. Just wasn't sure after today."

"What do you mean today?" he barked. "She *told* you?! That blasted woman can't keep her tongue still for one minute!" Heat rose from the skillet but it was no match for the fury that coursed through his veins. Fury at his own embarrassment more than anything.

"Whoa, whoa, whoa," Rory interrupted. "What are you talking about? I was talking about your tour of the gallery. I hadn't heard from you so I just assumed you didn't like what you saw today, and I didn't know if that would be awkward for you tomorrow around Caroline."

"What?" Finn focused on what she had just said. "The gallery?"

"Yeah, you toured the gallery earlier today..." she prodded.

"Oh, right. Yes. I did. It's fine."

"But you aren't. What's going on? Why are you mad at Caroline?"

"When am I not?"

"True, she does seem to crawl under your skin. Did she just leave or something?"

"I don't want to talk about it."

"Come on, Finn, you were threatening to murder the poor woman. What did she do? Should I ask her not to come tomorrow?"

Rory's loyalty to him had him smiling. It didn't matter that his sister liked Caroline and hoped to establish a friendship. If the woman crossed him, his little sister's fierce loyalty sided with him without hesitation.

"No. She's fine. She just..." he tried to think of something to say. "She just walked into my shop again. You two are becoming unreasonable."

Rory laughed. "Then put a lock on the door!"

"That's what she suggested."

"Smart woman."

"Or you two could just steer clear of here and let me work." His tone lightened as they bantered back and forth and the conversation ended with Rory's infectious laughter, a sound he truly loved.

Suddenly in a better mood, he added blended eggs to the skillet with some peppers. Apparently, he was making an omelet. He shook his head in dismay. Caroline had him so messed up in the head he didn't even have control over his own actions. He wasn't even aware he was making dinner. Turning off the burner and sliding the omelet onto a plate, he set it aside. He wasn't even hungry. All he could think about was her. And knowing that, and hating himself for it, he knew the only thing that would take his mind off of her was his glass. Pulling a beer from the refrigerator to take with him, he braced himself for what he knew would be another long night in the shop.

∞

Caroline pulled into the drive of a quaint adobe home on the outskirts of Santa Fe, surrounded by a picturesque yard and neighborhood meant for families and retired folks. The house suited Rory, with its impressive front entry and giant floor to ceiling window the focus instead of the front door. The sun bounced off the glass and were it not for the heavy landscaping surrounding the front porch, it would have spotlighted whomever walked up the path. Instead, its bright spark of reflection filtered through leaves and blossoms of crepe myrtles that lined the walkway. She reached the door as it swung open and Dan stood with a welcoming smile. "Perfect timing, Caroline. I was just about to grab something out of my truck. Come on inside. Rory is in the kitchen." He pointed the direction and she walked inside. The neutrality of the décor surprised her until she walked through the living room and spotted an enormous glass sculpture of obsidian and purple centered on the mantle of the fireplace, the glass twisting and rising towards the ceiling. It was one of Finn's, and if Rory Graves could be captured in glass form, this is how she'd look. The sculpture looked more like tentacles reaching up from the ocean bottom, but the passion, the colors, the spunk to the piece captured her new friend well.

"One of my many gifts from my brother. He spoils me."

Caroline turned and accepted the warm hug from Rory.

"So glad you're here. Come on, I'll introduce you to everyone."

She pulled Caroline by the hand until they reached a bright and open kitchen. All the faces were unfamiliar minus one. Her gaze found Finn's and he immediately looked down at his drink.

"Everyone," Rory announced. "This is Caroline."

Everyone greeted her in unison. "Finn, hook Caroline up with a drink, won't you?" Rory nudged Caroline his direction and then scampered back to whatever conversation she had previously come from. Caroline felt her heavy footsteps trudge their way towards Finn, the obvious discomfort of her presence evident on his face. He handed her a glass filled with tea. "It's not sweet," he stated.

"That's fine."

"If you want it sweet, then you can add something from the table." He pointed to a small container holding a variety of sweetners.

"Hello there." An older woman with a brilliant smile and short cropped hair the same black color as Rory's sculpture walked up, her eyes surveying Finn and then Caroline. "I'm Lyn Walsh, Rory and Finnegan's mom." She extended her hand and

Caroline accepted it with a smile. "Caroline Pritchard."

"And how do you know my kiddos?" she asked, looking to her son for explanation but not finding one.

"We met through Matilda, actually, from Frank's."

"Frank's Bistro, yes!" Lyn grinned. "Matilda and Frank should be here soon as well. So how do you know them?"

"I work on their street and eat there quite frequently. Matilda welcomed me from the start."

"That's her way." Lyn nodded as she spoke and then looked to her son again, whose attention, she realized, was on anyone and anything but the woman beside him.

"And you met Finnegan through Matilda?"

"Actually no, Rory introduced us."

"Did she now?" Intrigued, Lyn stepped closer to them as she moved out of the way of Dan as he entered and headed towards Rory.

"Well, Finnegan, Rory tells me you agreed to an art exhibition show. Why did you not tell me this the other day when I telephoned you?" In true motherly form, she tilted her head towards him and narrowed her eyes until the truth would come out.

He shrugged and she swatted him on the shoulder, surprising him and Caroline. "You oaf," she cackled as she linked her arm with his and laid her head gently against his arm. "Don't you know your mother needs to know these things so she can brag about you to all her friends?"

"Exactly why I did not tell you, Mom."

"Oh you..." She rolled her eyes and looked to Caroline and beamed proudly. "My son is an artist, has he told you?"

"Actually yes, I've seen his shop."

Astonished, Lyn looked to Finn for explanation and then back to Caroline. "Really?" Baffled, she switched from Finn's arm to Caroline's. "And you survived?"

Caroline laughed, the two women glancing at Finn as he purposely ignored them.

"Barely," Caroline admitted. "But I did convince him to do the art show at the Daulton... somehow." She threw up her hands as if still unsure how she managed such a feat.

"The Daulton Gallery on Canyon Road?" Lyn asked.

"Yes ma'am. I'm the new gallery manager there and I stumbled across Finn's glasswork and tracked him down. Well, Matilda helped me with that and sent me Rory's direction."

"So you're Johnny's replacement over at the Daulton? How about that?" She looked up at Finn and noticed he was slowly slipping away to make an exit. She gripped his arm and tugged so as to drive her point home that he was not to leave the conversation just yet. "I will have to tell my husband. Not sure if Rory and Finnegan told you, but we exhibit all over Santa Fe."

"Rory did, yes. I have seen some of your collection."

"Well, if you ever need filler pieces or just wish to have an eclectic bunch, you just let me know," she winked. "We've displayed at the Daulton in the past, but it's been years ago." She gently hugged Finn's arm and squeezed. "I'm so proud that you will be showcased there, sweetie. What an honor."

"It was Rory's doing."

"But it's your art." She patted his arm.

Finn tried to free his arm but his mother held tight. "And what a great person to work with," she continued, nodding towards Caroline. "You seem like a good fit, Caroline. The Daulton needed a bit of a shake up."

"Thank you, Mrs. Walsh."

"Oh, please, call me Lyn! After all, I'm sure we will be seeing more of one another. I would not miss my son's art show for the world. You know, it's been years since he's done one. He hoards his art like a priest with confessions."

"Oh, I am aware." Caroline laughed as she tapped Finn on the back in a friendly pat, the touch and the fact Finn did not jump away had his mother's brows rising.

"Well, I am so pleased he committed to you for the show. When is it scheduled?"

"Second Friday in August," Caroline explained.

"Well put me down on the invites, because I will not be missing it."

"Of course. If the rest of his pieces are as stunning as the focal sculpture, everyone will be in for a big treat."

"Oh, did you create a new piece?" his mother asked, looking to Finn.

"Yes," he replied. "Excuse me." He set his glass on the table and walked away, heading towards Dan and Rory.

"That boy." Lyn shook her head. "I apologize for his rudeness, Caroline. He—"

"No worries. I'm familiar with it already."

Lyn turned to the petite blonde beside her and saw her watching Finn from across the room. The tenderness in her gaze had Lyn's lips twitching into a smile. Not many people appreciated Finnegan's lack of social grace, but it seemed Caroline Pritchard did not mind at all.

«CHAPTER EIGHT»

"*I see Mom has roped* Caroline in for the long spiel about how great and wonderful her children are." Rory took a sip of her tea as she and Finn eyed their mother suspiciously.

"That she has."

"She's a good sport." Rory set her glass on the counter as several more of her friends began flooding into the room. Loud voices, greetings, hugs, and excitement buzzed throughout the room and Finn started feeling suffocated. He nodded a polite greeting to those he'd met before, and he avoided those he hadn't. He side stepped around another group and had almost made it to the back door when Caroline stepped in his path. "Hey."

He scowled down at her. "I need some air."

Understanding flashed on her face and she stepped out of the way as he headed outside. She followed. Naturally.

"You okay?" she asked, as she watched him place his hands on the railing and look out over the yard.

"Fine."

She placed a hand on his back as she stepped up next to him and he whirled. "Don't touch me."

She quickly drew back her hand as if bitten. "I'm sorry, I was just trying to—"

"Well don't. I came out here for air and to be alone, Caroline."

"And maybe I came out here because I was feeling uncomfortable surrounded by people I don't know and wanted to hang around the one person I do know. Somewhat. Vaguely," she added.

"I don't want company right now."

"Too bad." She leaned on the railing as well and fell quiet. Though she didn't speak, *for once*, he thought, her presence shouted at him. Again, he found himself drawn to her silky hair and delicate features. The soft curve of her cheek. The faint blush to her face, probably from temper towards him. The fact she stood next to him even after he barked at her.

"Your mom is nice."

He turned towards her, exasperation on his face and she grinned wickedly as if knowing his annoyance with her disruption would irritate him. Instead of reacting how she expected him to, he nodded.

"She's awfully proud of you," Caroline continued, challenging herself to get him to talking. Finn didn't respond.

"I haven't met your dad yet, but you favor him." Still no response. Finn's gaze still stared out at the yard, his elbows resting on the porch railing as he leaned forward.

Caroline drummed her fingers against her chin and then turned, her back resting against the railing so she could stare at his face better. His watchful eyes darted to hers for a brief second before moving back to the yard. She grinned, knowing he couldn't stand the fact she stared at him. "So about yesterday…" she began.

"Enough." He stood and she pointed up at him.

"Aha!" She gleefully danced in place as she hit his arm and laughed. "You cracked. I knew if I kept at it you would speak finally."

He shook his head as she continued bragging about her success.

"Don't get cocky." His statement drawing forth more giggles and laughs that were contagious in spite of his best efforts and soon had him smiling at her. He reached out and swiped a tear from her face as she tried to stop the belly laughs.

Inside, Lyn stood watching the interaction and snagged Rory's arm as she passed by. "Is that our Finn?"

Rory focused on her brother's amusement at Caroline and the interaction between the two. His shoulders relaxed, his handsome face spread into a smile, and his eyes only focused upon the woman in front of him, Rory's eyes brightened. "Looks like him."

"I've never seen him act that way with anyone." Breathless at the discovery, she reached for her husband. "Peter," she pulled him next to her and Rory and pointed through the glass door. "Look at our son."

At that moment, Finn threw his head back and roared with laughter as Caroline spoke with animated hand gestures. She rested her hand on his arm as she continued telling some story and Finn did not shy away from her touch.

"Who's the woman?" Peter asked.

Rory and her mother grinned. "Caroline," they said in unison.

"Hmm, interesting." Peter acknowledged his son's curious behavior, but unlike the women, moved on and didn't think anything more of it.

∞

Hearing the sound of clapping, Caroline looked inside and noticed Rory gathering everyone together in the kitchen. "I think we are to go listen now." She pointed and Finn turned to see his sister wave him inside.

"Guess so."

Caroline started forward and he grabbed her arm. She paused, looking down at his touch and then up at him. "Thanks for talking with me."

She smiled and then tilted her head towards the house for him to follow her. When they entered, the room was crowded, the barbecue dishes and sides spread out on the kitchen bar, and everyone stood around waiting to dive into the delicious food.

"Before we all eat," Rory began, as she stepped closer to Dan and snuggled into his side, her arm draped lovingly around his waist. "Dan and I have an announcement." They grinned at one another before looking at all their friends and family.

"For several years, we have tried to get pregnant." A few gasps sounded around the room and had

Rory's smile widening. "Unfortunately, all our attempts failed."

Confusion swept over the crowd and had her bouncing in excitement.

Dan picked up where she left off. "We've decided to adopt."

Everyone clapped and surprise fluttered around the room, and Caroline looked at Finn. He showed no surprise to the announcement and she wondered how long he'd known. Dan held up his hand for silence once more so Rory could continue.

"We've gone through all the steps and are on the list to adopt from birth. And normally this process can take years before we find a birth mother who will choose us. But we had our home study visit and we were placed on the list six months ago."

Lyn swiped a napkin under her eyes as Peter rubbed small soothing circles on her back as their daughter continued.

"And we were chosen last week by a birth mother!"

Everyone cheered and Rory began crying as she accepted hugs and teary well wishes from the crowd.

"How exciting!" Caroline looked up at him and saw his jaw tense. "Finn?" she asked. "You okay?" She brushed her hand over his arm and he jerked to attention.

"I'm fine."

"Did you know about all this?" Caroline asked.

"Just that they planned to adopt. I didn't realize they had already been chosen."

She continued studying him and he finally looked down at her. "I'm happy for them."

Nodding, she offered a smile. "You're going to be an uncle."

His eyes widened at that thought and he grew nervous about the idea of a small child wanting to rummage around his house and potentially break his glass. He cringed.

"Uh oh," Caroline teased. "Did I ruin the moment? Too much too soon?"

He shook his head. "It will be fine."

"Fine?" she asked on a laugh.

"Well, kids are... messy and clumsy. He won't be allowed to come to my house until he's older."

She laughed. "First off, how do you know it will be a boy? Second, good luck with that. Something tells me the kid will want to visit your house all the time."

"Why is that?"

"Because you have more space to run and play outside. It's like a playground for a kid's imagination."

"Joy."

"Don't act so disgusted. Kids are fun."

Rory walked up to him and hugged him. Pulling back she cupped his face. "I didn't tell you the news last week because I wanted it to be a surprise for everyone at the same time. But I wanted to thank you again for making it all possible, big brother." She kissed him on the cheek and hugged him tightly before wandering away once more.

"What did you do to make this all possible?" Caroline asked.

"Nothing. Absolutely nothing."

"Obviously something," Caroline nudged him and noticed the free-spirited Finn had retreated and he was back inside his hard shell. She dropped her questions and ventured towards Lyn, who accepted her with open arms and hugged her in her excitement as well. When Caroline glanced towards the back door, Finn was gone.

∞

"So here is where we will place 'Beautiful Fury,'" Caroline explained to Rory as she pointed to a round marble table in the center of the gallery's grand hall. The position was perfect, the overhead skylight would allow natural light to shine through the piece until the sun went down. Then, the various spotlights would take over the work of illuminating the piece.

Rory glanced at her watch and sighed. "Sorry he is late."

Caroline waved away her worry as she continued walking around the room explaining her ideas for the art exhibit to Rory.

"He didn't answer his phone this morning, but I know he got my message, because he always checks them every hour if he's working."

"You worried something's happened?"

"No. I know he's fine in regards to safety. He's just been avoiding me since we made our announcement the other day."

"Why would he do that?"

"He's embarrassed."

"Whatever for?" Caroline motioned towards her office and Rory plopped into one of the chairs across from her. "Because I told everyone he helped us."

"Helped you?"

"Well, yeah," she waved her hand towards the gallery. "The only reason he agreed to do this art show was so Dan and I could choose what avenue of adoption we wanted to pursue. To choose an adoption straight from birth is actually a little more costly than other options. Finn realized we could use the extra income and agreed to do the show so I could earn some extra commissions."

"That's why he bartered with me about the gallery's cut." Caroline realized and her heart softened at the thought of him trying to earn more for his little sister.

"He what?" Rory asked.

"Well, he wasn't happy with the thirty percent you and I had agreed upon, so we bartered down to fifteen percent. It was the only way I could get him to sign the contract."

Baffled, Rory shook her head. "That jerk didn't even tell me." She smiled and then rolled her eyes. "Typical."

"He's probably not avoiding you; he has probably just been swamped in his shop working."

"True." She leaned eagerly forward as a shadow gave way to a person standing in Caroline's doorway and Finn stood, hands carrying a small vase of roses. "You're late," she commented, eyeing him as he walked inside the small space and handed the vase to Caroline.

Fumbling a bit in surprise, Caroline held the delicate vase and smelled the roses. "Are these for me?"

"Who else would they be for?" he asked, as he nudged Rory's ankles out of the way and crossed to the open chair next to her.

"Thank you," Caroline whispered as she eyed him with a sweet smile.

He pointed to the vase and she looked it over. It was an odd shape, she realized. One curve of the bottom hung awkwardly lower than the other side, and the neck arched in a sway to offset the curvature of the base. But the colors were stunning.

"Recognize it?" he asked.

Pure joy radiated from her face as she held it up for Rory to see it. "My vase! This is my vase!"

Finn suppressed his smile at her excitement over the homely piece and watched as she had the audacity to set it beside 'Beautiful Fury' on a table behind her desk.

"I made that," she proudly told Rory as she motioned over her shoulder.

"You *made* it?" Rory asked, eyeing her brother closely.

"Well, Finn helped me, but yes, I made it." Caroline looked to Finn to vouch for her story and he shook his head. She frowned.

"I cannot take credit for that."

Rory laughed as Caroline folded her arms across her chest and looked the vase over. "So it's not perfect," she began and bit back a giggle. "But it has character."

"It sure does!" Rory agreed. "I can't believe he let you work in his shop. I haven't even gotten to do that."

"Really?" Caroline asked in surprise and looked to Finn. "Well, maybe we can do it again and you can make one too."

"That'd be awesome! Or we could have actual classes out at his place! People would pay big money to be taught by F.W.!" Both women turned towards Finn in excitement and he held up his hands.

"You are not invading my shop... again. No one touches my tools. No one touches my glass."

"But you let Caroline," Rory pleaded in a false whine.

"And it was obviously a mistake because it has planted hare-brained ideas into your heads."

"Just think of all the people," Caroline continued looking to Rory.

"*SO* many people," Rory agreed in jest. "Just wanting to hang out with you, big brother." She patted his leg and he stood.

"I'm leaving now."

Both women pleaded for him to stay as they laughed at his sheer determination to exit the room of awful ideas.

"We are just kidding, Finn, wait!" Caroline jumped from her seat and chased him down the hall. She grabbed his arm and he spun around, but instead of a sharp attack, his eyes held amusement.

"We are totally kidding."

"I know. Just thought it best to leave before I caved into participating in something I do not want to."

"Oh." She grinned and stuck a hand on her hip. "So does that mean you're open to the idea of tours to your shop?"

"Absolutely not."

She snorted and laughed.

"I brought you some pieces," he said. "I'll go get them."

Caroline watched him with a sloppy smile on her face as she leaned against the wall.

"You're falling for my brother, aren't you?" Rory's head poked out of the doorway, her rear end still occupying the chair in Caroline's office as she sat doing her sisterly duty of spying.

Caroline flushed. "No, not at all. I am just grateful Finn and I can work together so well now."

"Right..." Rory pointed a finger at her and then ducked back into the office urging Caroline to find her way back behind her desk.

"Although, to his credit, Finn is a much nicer guy than he lets on," Caroline admitted.

"He's one of those multi-layer types," Rory explained. "He doesn't like too many people around him. He doesn't allow many to grow close to him."

"Why is he like that? Did something happen to cause him to want to shut people out?"

"Not that I can remember," Rory said. "He's just always been one to like his space." She fished in her purse for a piece of chewing gum. "In fact, this one time, I was around nine and Finn was about thirteen. I had a sleepover. Just a few of the girls from school, my first sleepover, super exciting stuff to a little girl. Well, my friends came over and we were having a blast making cookies with my mom when Finn and my dad walked into the house from fishing. Finn's face, I'll never forget it," she paused a moment. "The shock, the fear, the disgust, all these different emotions played across his face as my friends began swooping in and trying to talk to him. I mean, he's a handsome guy, I get it. And even then, he was a cute kid. Well, a cute boy landing in the middle of a crowd of young girls... let's just say he started panicking. He ended up dropping his rod and reel and bolting out the door. That was the night of his first anxiety attack. My dad found him on the dock, just lying there. Thankfully, he came to pretty quickly, but that night forever changed the way we operated as a family. I no longer had sleepovers after that. His social interactions grew slimmer, our social interactions grew slimmer as a family. It was too much for him." She shrugged her shoulders. "He was always a closed off kid growing up, but when he found his craft it was as if he awoke from a deep sleep. It ignited something inside him. Believe it or not, the Finn now is much more interactive than the Finn of yesteryear."

Caroline could not comprehend that one at all. Though she had made some progress with Finn, the man was still a recluse and highly prized his privacy. She didn't know much about him other than what she'd learned from Rory. The only time she felt she truly knew Finn was when she worked with him in his shop. Like Rory said, he came alive when his hands were creating.

"Where do you want them?" Finn's voice had them both jumping as the two women hopped to their feet and joined him in the lobby. Caroline gasped as she eyed all the wooden crates, big and small, spread out over the lobby. Ed worked his way through the door with another load, and Finn held the door for him.

"What—" Caroline's words trailed off as she looked at Finn in wonder. "Are these from your shelves?"

"Some. The rest are what I've made the last week."

"I'm amazed, Finn."

"Don't be. It's my job."

Rory rolled her eyes at his reply as she watched Caroline admire her brother's work and then her brother.

"Ms. Caroline, where do you want me to take all this?"

The stars in Caroline's eyes cleared as she turned to her maintenance man. "The storage rooms are fine, Ed, thank you. I will come back there to unbox, photograph, and catalog the individual pieces later today."

"Yes ma'am." He carried his first load through the lobby and Finn reached to grab two crates to follow.

Caroline grabbed his elbow. "You still have an entire month before the show, Finn, you didn't have to rush and bring me your work."

His hands full, he looked down at her. "I didn't want you hounding me about it, or worse, coming to my shop."

She huffed in annoyance. "Yeah, okay, go." She motioned for him to follow Ed and threw her hands up in forfeit as Rory sat at a chair in the entry hall waiting for her.

"Lunch?" Rory asked.

"Yes, please." Caroline was still shaking her head when Finn came back to the foyer to retrieve more pieces.

"Meet us at Frank's when you're done, Finn." Rory commanded.

"Maybe." He walked passed Caroline with another load and avoided eye contact.

«CHAPTER NINE»

Rory opened the door and Caroline welcomed the fresh air on their short walk to Frank's, the slight breeze cooling her flushed cheeks and settling her erratic emotions. They sat at their usual table. "I can't believe he brought that many pieces already." Caroline said, as she tried to decide what sounded good to eat. She accepted the fresh glass of lemonade Matilda brought over with a warm welcome and then looked to Rory. "Do you really think I annoy him that much? I mean, after you told me about his previous experience with a gallery owner and how terrible it turned out, I've honestly tried to be as professional and kind as possible. Not rushing him or hounding him."

"I think," Rory began and leaned back in her chair resting her coral colored sandal on the seat of the chair next to her before continuing. "Finn likes ruffling your feathers."

"Why?"

"Because I think he likes you."

"Well, I'm glad he does, but I don't want him to feel pressured or that the gallery is hovering over him."

"First off, I don't think it has anything to do with the gallery hovering. I think he actually likes *your* hovering."

A blush stained Caroline's cheeks as she looked at her menu.

"Did I hit a nerve?"

"Of course not. The idea is absurd."

Rory caught the lack of belief in Caroline's tone and crossed her arms. "What's going on, Caroline?"

"What do you mean?" Caroline took a sip of her lemonade and diverted her eyes to the sidewalk.

"Did something happen between you and Finn? Did he insult you?"

"No, nothing like that." Caroline waved away Rory's concern. "Nothing has happened, Rory."

"Are you sure? Because the other day at the barbecue you two seemed pretty chummy. And then he brought you flowers today."

"I didn't know anyone else at the barbecue," Caroline whispered across the table as if she did not want anyone overhearing their conversation. "And he only brought me flowers because he brought me my vase."

"But he allowed you in his shop. He allowed you to touch his glass and tools. He let you work with him. He brought you a vase, but took the time to buy roses to fill it. He shows up with half his exhibit completed. He designs the most stunning piece of his career and drops it off at your office. The list goes on and on, Caroline. These behaviors are uncommon for Finn."

"They are all professional interactions, Rory. Let's not get carried away."

"Then," Rory continued and had Caroline blushing and fidgeting in her seat. "At the barbecue you two were in your own world on my back porch, and you had him laughing and smiling so effortlessly."

"And then he left without even saying goodbye and hasn't contacted me until walking into the gallery earlier," Caroline finished in a harsh whisper. "So by my accounts, it all means nothing. He interacts with me when he needs to. That's it." She saw Finn walking up the sidewalk and followed him with her gaze. Her pulse reacted immediately and she kicked herself for responding to him in that manner. "Now let's end this conversation because he's about to join us."

"I still smell something fishy," Rory said, and she watched as Caroline welcomed Finn to the table. He sat and then immediately stood again.

"Be right back. I need to talk to Frank." He moved off and towards the kitchen, Matilda waving him on back.

"And he's joining us for lunch in a public place." Rory began nagging again, only louder, "He never does that. Not even with me. And—"

"Oh alright! He kissed me!" Caroline threw up her hands, her face flushed with annoyance as her voice carried towards the surrounding tables and had her cheeks flaming and her eyes nervously darting towards the kitchen. Thankfully, Finn remained inside.

Rory, mouth agape, stared at her like she'd grown an extra head.

"He what?"

"You heard me."

"When?" Rory grinned as she leaned forward, eager to hear more.

"The other day at his house. The day I made the vase. Look," she held her hand out to try and tame

Rory's excitement. "It was an accident. He didn't mean to. It just sort of happened."

"He didn't mean to? How does someone not mean to kiss another person's lips? That doesn't even make sense."

"What I mean is, he did... it, and then was mad at himself and walked away. He hasn't mentioned it since, so I think it was just all a misunderstanding and a mistake."

"Have you tried talking to him about it?"

"No. Of course not."

"Of course not." Rory shook her head in dismay. "You two are going to be the death of me, I know it." She rubbed her fingers over her eyes as if warding off a headache. Finn slipped back into his chair and grabbed Rory's lemonade. Caroline avoided his gaze.

"What did I miss?"

"Nothing much," Rory said. "So you kissed Caroline?"

He choked on his lemonade and as he turned to scold Caroline, all he caught was her embarrassed face as she bolted to her feet and hurried down the sidewalk without a backward glance.

∞

"Way to go, Rory." Finn accepted the food item before him and thanked Matilda as he popped a fry into his mouth.

"What? Someone needed to bring it up."

"Why?"

"Because you two never would and I could tell something was going on between the two of you. You know how hard it was to pry that out of her? So tell me, why'd you kiss her, Finn?" Rory wriggled her eyebrows.

Sighing, Finn shook his head. "I don't think it kind to discuss the matter with anyone but Caroline. And since it was an accident—"

"Don't use that line. Kissing is never an accident," Rory stated, the exasperation evident in her voice. "When did you start having feelings for her?"

"I don't."

"So you just kiss random women now? When did this come about? Because I have to admit, I'm a little surprised that the man passed out in his truck a few weeks ago from people crowding him and touching him just randomly kisses different women."

"That's enough." His voice grew dark.

"I don't see why you're getting upset about it. You two obviously have some chemistry. I've never seen you act the way you do when you're around her. So what is it about Caroline that has you kissing her on 'accident?'" Rory asked, punctuating the question with air quotes.

"I do not have to answer that. It's my business. And Caroline's."

"Is it because you two haven't talked about it?"

"No."

"Really? Because she said you haven't."

Finn tossed the remaining part of his sandwich on his plate and began wiping his hands on his napkin. "This conversation is finished."

"I'm not trying to make you mad, Finn."

"You're pestering me. And you are doing it on purpose."

"True. But I am also trying to look out for you."

"I don't need someone to look out for me. I'm the big brother, that's my job. And I certainly do not need someone looking after me in regards to Caroline. I can handle Caroline."

"Obviously," Rory whispered behind her glass as she grinned.

Growling in irritation, Finn stood. "I should go check on her."

Rory snapped her fingers at him. "See, that right there. Empathy. When did you start caring about other people?"

"I care about lots of people." He pointed at her before tossing a few bills on the table. "Mind your own business, Rory, before it gets you into trouble."

∞

Finn did not head straight to the Daulton after lunch. He needed time to process what exactly happened and what he would even say to Caroline when he did see her next. Obviously, he would apologize for his nosy younger sister. But how would he bring up the subject of his kissing her and not feel completely like a jerk or an oaf? He shouldn't have done it, that's what should have happened.

He spent the remainder of his day touring other galleries on Canyon Road to see what attention they paid to glass artists. He visited the Longworth Gallery, Tansey Contemporary, Vivo Contemporary, Wiford Gallery, and La Mesa of Santa Fe. Most were contemporary art galleries, but he did not see one that featured a glass artist in their own showcase. *His would definitely be different*, he thought. And what Caroline had planned would stand out amongst the rest of the galleries for sure.

They had agreed that his glass would be displayed for a month after the exhibit. The pieces that did not sell that evening would be displayed, along with new pieces he wished to contribute for the remaining month following. Having such a brief follow up availability would place a sense of urgency on the patrons to purchase the evening of the exhibition instead of waiting. He liked the concept. And since Rory's adoption seemed to be fast tracked, he hoped his sister would have what she needed sooner rather than later.

He opened the door to the Daulton after five o' clock and poked his head into her office only to find it empty. He wound his way through the rooms back to the storage area and heard voices.

"Now you don't have to process this all right now, Ms. Caroline," Ed's voice carried through the narrow room, the shelves full of artifacts, pottery, tapestries, and the like blocking Finn's view of Caroline.

"I know, Ed. I just want to get a head start."

"Alrighty. Well, I'm going to head home. I'll see you in the morning, Ms. Caroline."

"Good night, Ed. See you tomorrow."

Finn stepped aside when Ed spotted him and offered a farewell nod on his way out. Finn leaned against the wall and watched her as she uncrated one of his smaller pieces. He heard her gasp at its beauty and watched as she tenderly polished it with a fine cloth. She smoothed her fingers over the elegantly blown tendrils and then polished away her smudges before placing it on a felt lined shelf. She moved to the next crate and snapped off the lid and reached inside. One of his large vases, the cylinder shape oblong and oversized for an everyday home, but perfect for a formal sitting room at a hotel lobby or place of business. She gasped again, and he heard a mutter of "Oh, Finn," as she lifted the piece carefully in her hands and turned it slowly as if memorizing every inch of it. She then set about her task of polishing away finger smudges and dust and set it on a shelf further down where he spotted several more of his vases. The care in which she worked, the appreciation for every single piece boosted his pride in his work in such a way that he wished he could only design for art lovers like her.

"You're working late." His voice boomed inside the small space and she jumped, thankfully not holding anything in her hands as she squealed.

She placed a hand on her heart. "You scared me."

"Sorry about that."

"What are you doing here?" She brushed the back of her hand over her forehead to wipe away the perspiration that had beaded there.

Faced with the moment he'd spent the last four hours rehearsing in his mind, he drew a blank. *What was he supposed to say again?*

"Finn?" she asked, slight annoyance tinging her words as she moved on to the next crate.

"You already unpacking them all?"

"Might as well." Her retort was quick and she avoided looking at him as she began polishing the next piece and placing it on the respective shelf.

"Do you always work late?"

"No."

"Then why are you working late this evening?"

"Because I want to," she replied with an easy shrug to her shoulders. "Is there something I can do for you?"

Avoiding her question he looked at all his pieces she'd unboxed. "You haven't moved 'Beautiful Fury' yet."

"No. It remains in my office for now."

"Why?"

She huffed, "Because I just haven't gotten to it, Finn. Is that alright?"

He held up his hands in surrender. "I didn't come to fight with you."

"Then why are you here?"

Honesty was the best policy. He hated that virtue and yet, he spoke before thinking. "I wanted to see you."

This had her head popping up, her eyes soft for a split second before she turned back to the crates. "I'm working."

"I can help. I'm pretty much an expert on this stuff." He waved his hand over his crates.

"I don't need help, but thank you."

He didn't listen, and instead, walked closer to her and noticed her retreating steps to the other side of the shelving unit so as to avoid him. His lips twitched.

"I'm sorry about Rory."

"What about her?"

"About her outburst earlier."

Caroline shrugged and moved an empty crate to the back of the room. When she walked by him, Finn clasped her wrist and felt her pulse jump beneath his fingers. "I came to talk to you."

"And I told you, I'm working. You can schedule a meeting with me for later in the week, but right now, I'm a bit busy."

"Don't give me that." His patience had begun to wear thin. Here he'd actually come to discuss what had begun to develop between them, or what he thought was developing, and she was blowing him off. Had he misread the situation? No. He felt her racing pulse. He saw the tenderness in her eyes when she looked at him, though she tried to hide it. He wasn't mistaken. She cared for him. And he had finally started feeling semi comfortable with that idea.

"Look, there's nothing to discuss. We were just caught up in the moment of a good ending to a good day. I understand. There's no need to let me down easy."

"I wasn't planning to."

Confused, Caroline tilted her head as she studied him. "Excuse me?"

"I didn't come to apologize for what happened between us."

"Okay..." she waited patiently as he fisted his hands in his pockets and stood in her path back to his crates.

"Look," he began, "I don't dislike you."

Her brows rose at his bold statement. "That's comforting to know."

Her sarcasm boiled his blood as he tried to maintain his calm composure. "I mean that I don't mind not disliking you."

"What?" Befuddled, she shook her head and squeezed her way passed him and headed back to her work.

Frustrated with himself, he hesitated a moment before following her. When he turned to pursue, she'd already returned and he bumped into her, a crate following to the floor.

"Finn!" she scolded, squatting down to open the crate to make sure the piece survived. She withdrew the lid and sighed. A small fracture line coursed through the piece. "You broke it."

"I can replace it." *Easy enough*, he thought.

"That's not the point," her voice rose. "I told you I am working. And instead of standing in my way and destroying pieces of art, maybe you could just leave. This conversation you wished to have is going nowhere anyway." She shoved past him again and he followed closer this time.

"I came here to talk to you." His voice was firm as it bounced about the empty gallery as she headed towards her office.

"Well maybe I don't want to talk right now." She grabbed her purse and flipped the light switch off as she made her way to the front of the building. "Stand here." She pointed to a spot and left him to key in a code in the alarm system. A beeping sound started counting down and she nudged him out the door and locked it behind them before walking towards her car in the parking lot. She clicked the locks and her lights flickered. "Why are you following me?" she asked.

"To discuss what happened at lunch." His own frustration billowed out as she spun on her heels her eyes bright with fury.

"I don't want to talk about it, okay?"

"Why are you mad at me?"

"I'm not mad!" Her voice shook as she spoke and he watched as she attempted to calm herself.

"I'm just not in the mood, Finn."

"Look, I said sorry about Rory's comment earlier."

"Oh, so I should feel fine then? Fine that she embarrassed me in front of you and everyone else at the bistro? Well, I'm not. I'm a bit aggravated, actually. And the last thing I want to do is talk about what happened between us when it's been over a week any way. Obviously it didn't mean anything or we would have already discussed it. And that's fine. It doesn't have to mean something.

I get it. I just don't want to hash this out right now because—"

"Because what?" he asked, sorry he'd ever stopped by the gallery.

"Because I think my feelings for you are a little skewed at the moment, and it's not professional of me to even consider those feelings right now. And personally, I'm not sure if I even want to have those feelings towards you in the first place."

He wasn't expecting her to unload her feelings on him. He wasn't expecting much of anything really. He honestly thought stopping by the gallery, visiting with her, and apologizing about Rory would put them back on solid ground where they were before. And he thought, miserably, he should have kept his mouth shut about the kiss. Because now, in all her fury and embarrassment, all he could think about was doing it again. Only he knew she would not welcome it.

That thought surprisingly disappointed him. And he remained standing in the lone parking lot as she backed away and left him standing on the gravel.

«CHAPTER TEN»

Two weeks had passed and Caroline had yet to see Finn since the night he barged into her back room at the gallery. *That was for the best,* she thought. She was able to focus on the exhibition show. Solely on the show. She rubbed the bridge of her nose as she scanned over the catalog and realized she was fooling herself. How was she not supposed to think of Finn when everything she looked at and talked about throughout the day was tied up in Finn? His work, his schedule, his shipments, his show. She was exhausted by all things Finn but yet still wanted to see more of him.

She and Rory had paved over the bistro mishap rather quickly. The spirited sister was hard to remain upset with and now Caroline classified Rory as a good friend. She received her Finn updates from Rory whenever she needed answers, but some questions weren't appropriate to ask. Like, how was he doing? Was he miserable without talking with her? She scoffed at her pathetic line of thinking as she saw Rory pull up next to the curb and pop her trunk. Another one of Finn's newest pieces. Caroline stepped outside to greet Rory and grinned as she reached into the trunk and pulled out two small crates. One had a ribbon tied around it, the other was plain like the previous crates.

"This one is for you. This one is for the show."

She handed the gifted crate to Caroline as she slammed her trunk closed and walked into the gallery. Both women headed straight for Caroline's office. Caroline set the crate aside and sat in her chair as Rory sat across from her.

"Aren't you going to open it?"

"Oh." Caroline reached for the crate and with nervous fingers untied the ribbon. "What's it for?"

Rory shrugged. "Finn didn't tell me. He just asked me to give it to you."

"That's odd." Caroline's brow furrowed as she looked to Rory.

Rory, shrugging again, sighed. "He's been acting weird since the day at the bistro. He said he came and talked with you. I assumed you guys smoothed everything out."

"Not sure if smooth would be the right word." Caroline lifted the lid and paused. The small sculpture, no taller than six inches was an exact replica of 'Beautiful Fury.' Touched, she reached for the small note next to it. *"So you will finally move the other one out of your office. F.W."*

She choked on a laugh as her eyes teared up and she placed the small sculpture on her desk. "He did not have to do this."

"Guess he wanted to."

"It's my favorite piece of his. If I could convince him, and also if I could afford it, I would buy that one." She pointed to the larger version behind her. "It just hits me right in the heart every time I look at it. Like a bolt of lightning. There's just something about it."

"And now you have a mini." Rory leaned forward to look at the sculpture. "He used to make me small figurines and such when he first started out. When he'd try a new technique he'd give me his guinea pig projects. I still have a few of them. Most of them have broken over the years though."

Caroline read the note again and smiled, her fingers lightly brushing the terrible handwriting.

Ed poked his head in the doorway. "Ms. Caroline, you're needed in the arch room. A couple has a question about your tapestry."

Nodding, Caroline rose. "I'll be right back."

Rory waved. "Take your time. I'm in no hurry."

As soon as Caroline stepped out, Rory reached for the note from her brother. What sweet message could he possibly have written to put such a look of love on Caroline's face? She read it and then rolled her eyes. *Only a woman in love would find that endearing,* she thought. Shaking her head, she messaged her brother:

RG: "You're such a weirdo."

FW: "Takes one to know one, sis."

RG: "She opened the sculpture."

FW: "And?"

RG: "Loved it. Why are you so nice?"

FW: "I'm always nice."

She shoved her phone away when Caroline walked back in. "So what's in that crate?"

Rory opened it and held up an opaque crystal sculpture tinged with silver.

"Wow. His work just continues to astound me," Caroline said as she admired the piece. "It's amazing to me how many ideas he comes up with."

"Don't boost his ego, please." Rory groaned. "Trust me, it's big enough."

"Have you been out there to see what else he's working on?"

"No. I haven't been over there for a while until last night. He told me to come back in a few days to collect the final pieces for the show."

"I could go collect them," Caroline offered, not trying to sound too eager, but she wanted to see him. *Needed to*, she realized. "I need to thank him for the sculpture and run a couple of things by him anyway."

"I'm not sure that is a good idea right now."

"Why?"

Rory grimaced. "He may have asked me to keep you away until after the show."

Offended, Caroline balked. "Why on Earth would he ask that?"

"He didn't say. But he is deep into his work right now, Caroline. Maybe he's trying to be as stress free as possible."

"And why would I stress him out?"

Rory sighed. "Listen, I'm just the messenger. I don't know what goes through my brother's head. All I know is that he's been working super hard lately to make this show a great one and he doesn't want any distractions. He threatened to feed me to the wolves the other day because I showed up for these two things. Like he asked me to, but it didn't matter. He did not want to visit or see me. So just let him have his space to work. After the show, I will let you deliver his payment and results, how about that?"

Dissatisfied, but willing to acquiesce, Caroline nodded. "If that's what he wants." She shot a gaze at her mini sculpture and brushed a finger over the smooth glass.

"Well, my work here is done, I guess." Rory stood.

"Wait, I haven't even asked you the status of your baby?"

An excited gleam hit Rory's eyes at her question. "We still have a little over a week or so. The doctor says the baby could come any day now, so we shall see. Dan is about to go crazy. He can't wait."

"And you still don't know the sex?"

"I didn't tell you?" Rory slapped a palm to her forehead.

Caroline shook her head.

"It's a girl."

Caroline clapped her hands and squealed as Rory danced towards her for a hug. The women embraced in excitement. "I'm so happy for you!"

"It's crazy." Rory stepped back and tucked her bangs behind her ear. "I mean, we could be parents in less than a week if the baby decides to come early."

"And the nursery?" Caroline asked.

"Is all ready to go. Dan has bought every gadget on the market that he thinks we will need."

"That's so sweet."

"I know." Rory placed a hand over her heart. "This process has truly made me love him even more. I didn't even think that was possible." Her eyes puddled and Caroline embraced her as her friend sniffled and then laughed.

"Agh, look at me." Rory pulled away and snatched a tissue off Caroline's desk. "I'm not even the one who's pregnant and I'm crying at everything."

"Happy tears are never a bad thing," Caroline encouraged. "It's a sign of your love for him and for your daughter."

"My daughter." Rory shook her head and smiled. "So crazy to think that will be true in just a few short days."

"Or couple of weeks," Caroline pointed out. "She could decide to draw out her arrival just to make you wait."

"Then she would be like her Uncle Finn," Rory piped back. "He's the worst at doing that." She walked to the door. "If I don't talk to you before, I'll see you in a few days with the final pieces."

"Sounds like a plan. I will be here." Caroline waved her hand around the gallery. "Making it gorgeous for Finn's big night."

"I know you will." Rory winked as she hopped into her car. "See ya!" she called, as she closed the door and set out down the street.

∞

He hammered down the lid of the last wooden crate to the last sculpture that would make its way to Daulton Gallery. To Caroline. Finn rubbed a hand over his lower back as he lifted the crate and set it outside his shop and shut the door. He was finished. And after such a feat, he decided he needed a beer and the weekend to relax his mind and his body. The hours he'd put in over the last few weeks had caught up to him and his hands ached from holding the pipe, his back was stiff from sitting in his chair, and every muscle in his body screamed from the tension that seemed to bundle him up as he worked. He could finally relax. The rest was up to Caroline and Rory.

He'd been updated on the gallery's preparations via Rory on her last visit, and it sounded like Caroline was creating a winning atmosphere. He hated the thought of not seeing it himself. He contemplated stopping by before the big event just to see the completed showcase, but he feared not being able to leave once he was there. And with his confusing feelings towards Caroline, he knew if she gazed up at him with those devastating green eyes, he'd give in. The thought twisted his insides and made him cringe at the pathetic reaction. The woman had him going crazy. He'd be lying to himself if he did not admit that most of his thoughts the last couple of weeks had been on Caroline. He created every piece in hopes that she would react much like she did when she unboxed his sculptures in the stock room. Or the way her entire being ignited at her first sight of 'Beautiful Fury.' He found that was one of his main motivations in the last couple of weeks. He wanted to knock Caroline's socks off. And he wanted her to have the largest turn out the Daulton had ever seen. Selfish? Yes. But he didn't care. The results were for Rory and Dan. And for Caroline. He wanted the Daulton to stand out amongst the other galleries on Canyon Road just as much as she did, and if his art could achieve that for her, then he was all in. He wanted success for her. He wanted to see her riding high on a successful showcase. Of course, he wanted to share in that excitement, but mostly, he wanted it for her.

He could no longer deny she'd weaseled her way past his defenses, but he still wasn't quite comfortable with the idea. He'd spent most of his life shunning people and avoiding them altogether. And though he found her fun company and not too bad to look at, he wasn't quite sure if he was ready to allow someone in. Someone close. Yes, she'd dealt with his anxiety before, but he knew the depth of that burden, and he wasn't sure if she or anyone else would want to share that burden with him forever. Or if anyone could fully understand it. And before Caroline, he was completely fine with handling his struggles on his own. Alone. He'd enjoyed being alone. He enjoyed working in his shop in silence. But now when he sat at his work bench he envisioned her across from him. The stool still sat where she had moved it. He hadn't taken the time to move it back against the wall, and he kept it where it was just in case she showed up again, ignoring his rule, and came inside to watch him work. He'd even found, on his longest days, that he hoped she would. But she never came. He had told Rory to keep her away, but he just knew Caroline would ignore the order at some point. But she hadn't. And now his workshop was haunted by the memory of her presence and it made him feel her absence even more.

He rubbed a hand over his face as he watched Rory's car speed up his driveway, a dirt tunnel swirling behind her as she took the last curve and headed directly towards his shop.

"I take it you are finished if you are out here for air?" she asked, as she swung her door closed and walked towards him. She smiled at the remaining crates settled around his feet. "Caroline is going to be so excited. I swear, she's like a kid on Christmas morning each time I bring one of these crates into the gallery. Her excitement has even rubbed off on Ed."

"I'm surprised she didn't come to collect them herself." Finn reached to pick up the first crate.

"Is that why you shaved?" Rory asked on a laugh as she darted ahead of him towards her car to open the trunk.

"Ha. Ha."

"Sorry to disappoint you, big brother, but that lady of yours is working her rear end off to make a beautiful exhibition show for you. She's been about like you: locking herself away, ignoring phone calls, and barely taking time to shower." She scrunched her nose as Finn brushed passed her.

"Sounds like it is coming together then." Finn hefted another crate and made the journey back to Rory's car.

"Yep. It's remarkable, Finn. Truly. You should sneak by there and take a look at it all. I would hate for you to miss seeing your work displayed in a gallery. And not just any gallery, but the Daulton. It is amazing what Caroline has done."

"No thanks."

"You're not even the least bit curious?"

"No."

"Liar." Rory could tell her brother was interested in hearing more. "'Beautiful Fury' looks incredible in the center room. I went by there this afternoon because Caroline called me in a tizzy."

"What happened to it?" Finn's head popped up and he braced himself for the bad news.

"Nothing. She was just taken aback by how gorgeous it looked with the sunlight beaming down through the domed window above it that she thought I needed to see it."

Finn exhaled in relief.

"And she was right, it was stunning. I all but had to drag her away from it to take her to lunch. I don't know when was the last time she'd eaten, but she scarfed down her sandwich at Frank's to hurry back over there to work." Rory studied him as he placed the last crate in her back seat. "You sure you don't want to come with me and take a look at it?"

"I'm sure."

"Finn," Rory sighed and placed a hand over his arm. "You have to see it." Her genuine plea did not fall on deaf ears. She could see a response in his eyes before he spoke.

"No."

Disappointed, Rory released his arm and walked towards her door. "I think it would mean a lot to Caroline if you swung by to see her hard work. She's taken a lot of pride in your showcase, Finnegan. The least you can do is show some appreciation."

"I'll think about it."

And she knew he would. Though he may not show up, Rory could see her brother battling over the idea already. She would not get her hopes up, as she warned Caroline not to as well. But fault her for life that she did hope, and prayed Finn wouldn't disappoint them both.

∞

All was in place. Each sculpture meticulously arranged in the perfect spot. The lights set to create a glorious shower of color throughout the entire gallery. The glass sparkled and dazzled all who entered, and about the time a breath could be drawn, the eyes would land on 'Beautiful Fury' and the air whooshed from the lungs and the heart leapt at the sight of such beauty. Caroline felt it each time she walked through the rooms, and she knew all the patrons would as well. It was astounding. The talent, the beauty— it all married inexorably to create a stunning masterpiece. She'd already fielded phone calls in regards to certain pieces based on the catalog alone. F.W. was a hit amongst art buyers and collectors not only from Santa Fe, but from across the country, and the exhibition show promised a turn out for the record books.

Caroline adjusted the base of one of the sculptures, the canary yellow glass swirling into the air in delicate tendrils made her think of warm sunshine tickling the skin. Smiling at the thought, she turned at the sound of footsteps. Rory grinned in welcome.

"I have the rest." She held up a crate and laughed as Caroline's eyes glossed over with tears of joy. "You are so delirious that the sight of a box makes you weepy. You need to rest, Caroline."

Caroline waved away the comment as she carried the box to the storage room to unbox whatever Finn had placed inside. She enjoyed this part the most. The unveiling of what lie beneath the lid, to unearth what beauty lay hidden in shadow. "Do I need to leave you two alone?" Rory's voice echoed through the room and had Caroline turning unamused.

"I'm just admiring the piece."

"You haven't even opened it yet," Rory pointed out.

"Well, I'm just taking a minute to imagine what could be inside. Excuse me for taking a moment to appreciate the wonder."

"Spoken like a true art nerd." Rory winked. "Finn would be pleased."

"I would hope he would be. My mother used to say there is no better compliment than appreciation for one's art. I wish Finn could see his work being admired," Caroline stated. "I don't think he realizes how it moves people. Though even if he did, he probably wouldn't care."

"I'm not so sure about that," Rory chimed in and had Caroline turning to face her. "I think Finn cares what people think, namely you. But he does not want the pressure of creating for other people. He creates for himself because then he does not have to worry about disappointing anyone but himself."

"Nothing he creates could disappoint," Caroline explained. "I wish he could see that."

"In time maybe he will." Rory smiled as Caroline gasped in pleasure at the sight of the round orb in her hands. She took a moment to stare into the crystal ball, the swirling colors swished throughout the clear center like a hidden galactic atmosphere. "He's never made anything like this,"

Rory whispered as she brushed a hand over the smooth curve of the sculpted ball.

"It's amazing." Caroline turned it in her hands to catch a ray of light from the window and both women gasped as small flecks of silver glinted from within and sparked radiant spots along the walls around them.

"It's like a secret." Rory bounced on her toes as she pulled Caroline's hands from the light and the ball was once again a beautiful sculpture. She then shoved it into the light and the ball illuminated the space around them once more. Both women giggled with excitement. "I'm in awe, and I've seen everything he's ever created. What's it titled?"

Caroline reached into the crate for Finn's note. "Santa Fe Sunrise."

"Perfection," she and Rory said at the same time.

"I asked him once when we were sitting on his deck steps if he drew inspiration from his surroundings. He seemed so aloof to the question I didn't think he was absorbing the beauty around him. How wrong I was." Caroline shook her head in disbelief as she held the breathtaking piece in her hands. "This needs a special spot."

Rory nodded in agreement. "You take care of that and I will unload the remaining pieces." She darted out of the room as Caroline walked around the gallery to plan where to place the magical orb.

Rory ran back into the room, arms empty and her face drenched of color.

"Rory?" Caroline placed the orb on a display shelf so as to take her friend's hands in hers. "What's the matter? Are you okay? What happened?" She started to lead Rory to a chair, but Rory shook her head.

"No, I can't. I have to go. I have to go!" Her voice rose. "That was the hospital. My baby..." her words trailed off and Caroline feared the worst. Before she could comfort her friend, Rory's face split into a smile. "She's coming! The baby is coming! I have to go! The crates are on the sidewalk. I'm sorry, Caroline, but I have to go!"

Laughing, Caroline hugged a bouncing Rory. "Go then! Go meet your daughter!"

Rory darted around the front of her car and opened her door. "Oh, the exhibition show!" She held a palm to her forehead.

"Don't worry about it. You welcome that little girl into the world and I will take care of things here. Now go!" Caroline waved her onward, Rory's excitement bringing joy to her face as her friend sped away. Basking in the joy of the moment, Caroline crossed her arms and eyed the remaining few pieces to be carried inside. She thought of Finn and wondered how he would accept the news of his niece's arrival. Would he go to the hospital? Would he hold the tiny baby? Would he want to?

She bent down and lifted two of the crates and carried them inside. It didn't matter how Finn reacted, she reminded herself. It was none of her business. The only business she needed to think about was his art. And if the showcase was to take place tomorrow evening, Caroline needed to wrap up the preparations. Sending a silent celebratory cheer to Rory and Dan, she set to work to create a memorable experience all her own.

«CHAPTER ELEVEN»

Rory paced in circles, Dan sat like a statue with his face in his hands, muttering prayers under his breath, and Finn's parents clasped hands and stood as close to the double doors leading to the delivery ward as was allowed. Finn sat and watched everyone experiencing the moment. The moment that would change all their lives, but mainly Rory and Dan's. He caught Rory's nervous gaze and offered an encouraging smile.

"How long does this take?" she asked the room, her mother smiling in sympathy.

"Sweetie, if she is anything like you, she will be here in a couple hours. If she's anything like your brother, however," his mother eyed him with mock annoyance. "She will take a whopping thirteen hours to make her arrival. Either way, she will be here soon." Lyn patted the seat next to her and Rory sat, leaning into her mother's warm and comforting embrace and thanking the heavens she had her entire family here for support.

Dan's head popped up and he flashed a panicked glance towards Finn. "I didn't install the car seat." He bolted to his feet and Peter intervened. "There's time for that later, Dan. Don't worry about it." Peter tried to maintain a sober expression as he patted his son in law on the back. "Babies can't leave the hospital right away any way."

"Oh, right. You're right." Dan's outburst muffled out and led right back to him sitting and praying. Rory reached for his hand and they huddled together, their undivided attention on one another and their future child. Finn felt a twinge of jealousy in that moment. Watching the love and acceptance merge into a beautiful picture of affection and tenderness, he immediately thought of his glass and what he would create to represent this particular moment. He'd gift it to the baby, of course, and it would be a piece of art capturing the excitement and the love her parents had for her. He'd have to make it pink, he reminded himself, remembering the rose colored, extravagantly girly nursery awaiting his soon-to- be niece.

The double doors opened and a nurse stepped out. Everyone's heads popped up and waited for her to speak. A smile spread across her face. "Would Mommy and Daddy like to come on back and meet their little girl?"

No one had to tell Rory and Dan twice. They hopped to their feet and accepted the help with hospital gowns and gloves to make their way back into the maternity unit. Lyn swiped her eyes and looked to Finn. "Can you believe it, Finnegan? Our Rory has a daughter."

Finn stood and walked over to sit next to his mother, knowing she needed to hold one of her own babies close as she waited to meet her new granddaughter. "I remember sitting in a room like this waiting for you." Peter rubbed his wife's back as he looked at Finn. "Your mother did not want me in the delivery room at the time."

"Oh, now Peter, it wasn't that I didn't want you there," Lyn admonished on a half sob of happy tears. "Your father almost fainted during the first contraction," she explained, "so the nurses thought it best for him to step out of the room." The two laughed softly at the memory and Finn felt, again, the small pangs of longing for a person to share such intimate moments with. His mind wandered to Caroline and whether or not she knew Rory would not be making the showcase tomorrow night. He would have to contact her and let her know the circumstances. His mom gasped and his attention was then focused upon Rory standing before them holding a small, pink wriggling blanket. Finn stood along with his parents and felt the air leave his lungs at the sight of the tiny human embraced in his sister's arms.

"Oh Rory," Lyn brushed a hand over the babies small beanie and hugged her daughter. "She's beautiful."

The baby started whimpering and Rory instinctively began to bounce and shush as she stepped towards Finn. "Say hey there, Uncle Finn," she grinned up at him as he stared down at the dainty little girl. One free hand emerged from the blankets, the tiny fingers stretching to test their capabilities before bunching into a tiny fist. He reached out and brushed his fingers over the soft skin and his heart melted.

"I'd like you all to meet Rosemary Finn Graves." Rory announced.

Finn looked at his sister and she beamed, a tear sliding down her cheek as he stood in surprise. He felt his own eyes cloud as he brushed his thumb over the tiny fist once more.

"Look," Rory whispered as she slid the small beanie off of Rosemary's head and revealed a full head of jet black hair. "She has hair like us."

Finn brushed a palm over the downy hair and bit back a soft laugh as he gazed upon the marvelous creation in wonder. "She does."

"I like to think she has my nose," Dan cut in and had everyone laughing.

"Poor kid," Finn responded and accepted the happy punch in the shoulder from the new dad.

Rory and Lyn gushed over the baby until the nurse emerged beckoning the new parents and baby back inside with the promise that visiting hours for Finn and his parents would be in another four hours. Lyn kissed Rory and Dan both on the cheek and brushed her hand over Rosemary's dark hair before stepping towards Peter's embrace to watch Rory walk back into the maternity ward. Rory waved at Finn and silently mouthed, "Thank you," as she walked into the next room.

∞

Caroline walked towards the Daulton, her heels digging into the gravel parking lot as she retrieved the gallery keys from her purse. Tonight was the night of F.W.'s exhibition showcase, and she wore her best black dress. Rory would not be here and neither would Finn. It was up to her to represent the artist and she would look and sound her best as she spoke with the patrons that were in attendance. She unlocked the doors to the Daulton and hurried to shut off the alarm before it sounded.

She heard a tap on the glass door and turned to see the catering crew. She unlocked the door to let them in and led them to the small kitchen they would be working out of. She glanced at the clock on the wall. *Two hours until go time*, she thought. She dropped her purse off in her office as she began flipping all the remaining lights to brighten up the gallery. Finn's glass sparkled to life and she inhaled a deep breath and prayed for a successful night. She did not want to let him down.

Two of Caroline's part time employees walked up, both dressed in black attire as well, and listened as she explained their roles for the evening. When she sent them off to their respective places, she then retrieved the clipboard that would house the purchase tickets and placed them on the podium in the corner of the main atrium, the room she would reside in most of the night giving her the luxury of gazing upon 'Beautiful Fury.' She circled around the sculpture making sure no dust, fingerprints, or obstructions could take away from its beauty. As always, the piece dazzled her. She loved the soft curves of the green silhouette and the harsh sharpness of the cobalt blue wave of angry shards. It was as if a woman were facing off with a force of nature and winning just by being herself. The way the blue did not overpower the green, more it slinked around its curves as if surrendering to its peace and beauty. She thought of the miniature version sitting in her office and then immediately thought of Finn. Again. She shook her head. She was here for his art tonight. She could think of the man later.

Waiters began scattering about the room at different posts with flutes of champagne and canapes. She heard the front door knock and walked forward to find the string quartet waiting to come inside. She let them in and escorted them to the atrium and watched patiently as they set up. The scene was set. And by the sounds of the front door opening and her employees greeting the first patrons, the showcase had begun.

Among the first to arrive were Lyn and Peter Walsh. After hugging Caroline for the hundredth time, Lyn accepted yet another tissue from her husband as she cried joyful tears over her son's beautiful work. "I just can't believe he agreed to do this. Look at this, Peter." She waved a hand over 'Beautiful Fury.' "It's glorious. Our son made this gorgeous piece."

"Did you doubt him?" Peter asked on a laugh.

"Of course not, I've just never seen something so beautiful." She smiled at Caroline and clasped her hand in hers. "Thank you, sweetie. This exhibit is truly astounding. I wish Finn and Rory were here to see it."

"Me too," Caroline admitted. "Though Rory has her own stunning piece of art to look at right now."

Lyn, the proud new grandmother gushed, "Oh, I know it. She is just the most beautiful little girl, Caroline. She looks as if she could be Rory's own daughter. Though, if she keeps up with her attitude, she will be more like her Uncle Finn." She chuckled as Caroline feigned a grimace.

"Then again, that may not be a bad thing if it creates such wonder as this." Caroline waved her hand around the room as more people filtered into the atrium. The collective gasps at the sight of 'Beautiful Fury' had her smiling. Peter wandered further into the gallery as Lyn stuck close to Caroline to comment on the reactions she witnessed from the patrons. She greeted a few by name and proudly announced to them the artist was her son, though she never mentioned his name.

Caroline listened as a woman indicated her desire to purchase one of Finn's sculptures and she filled out the ticket with the woman's information and then walked the "sold" notice over to the piece and set the placeholder in front of it.

"That's a good sign."

She jumped in surprise and turned to find a nervous Finn standing behind her, dressed in a black tux with navy tie and his hands in his pockets. "Finn?"

"Who else would it be?" He tried to bite back a grin at her shock, but his lips twitched into a smile.

Caroline placed her hand on her heart as she tried to catch her breath. Her eyes held his and slowly her face relaxed into a beaming smile up at him. She linked her arm with his. "I'm so glad you came," she whispered. "I can't believe you came." She looked up at him and noticed his steel gaze surveying his surroundings.

"Ms. Pritchard," an elderly man's voice interrupted her study of Finn as she turned to the gentleman.

"Yes?"

"The sculpture in the atrium. I wish to place a bid."

"Oh, I'm sorry sir, but that one is not for sale. It is just a statement piece for tonight."

"I wish to make a bid any way. Should the artist choose to sell, I want to be first on the list."

"It's not for sale." Finn added in a harsh whisper and had Caroline tightening her hold on his arm.

"Of course. Rachel is at the podium and will accept your bid, sir. Though I cannot promise the artist will accept it."

"Very well. Thank you." He turned and walked towards the podium in the other room.

"It's not for sale," Finn repeated to her.

"I know, but it makes him feel better knowing he potentially has a say in a piece. He'll end up purchasing two of your pieces that he can."

"You sound confident."

"Let's just say I know his type."

"Thanks for not telling him I was the artist."

She looked up at him and she swore she saw his gaze soften as it swept over her face. "I didn't want you storming out just as you arrived."

He smirked at that and allowed her to lead him from room to room.

Lyn spotted them and rushed towards them, enveloping Finn in a tight embrace of proud parent. Peter clapped him on the back.

"Oh, Finnegan," Lyn stared up at him in pure parental joy. "Isn't it just stunning? Didn't Caroline just bring it all to life?"

He nodded. "Glad you guys came."

"Oh honey, we wouldn't have missed this for the world. We are so proud of you." She whispered so as not to be overheard. "And I'm even more proud that you came." Her gaze followed Caroline as she watched her place another placeholder in front of a piece and secretly cast Finn a thumbs up before helping another patron.

"She truly is marvelous, isn't she?" Lyn commented, studying her son as he watched the beautiful woman in the slim black dress. All she received was a grunt of agreement as Finn followed Caroline with his eyes as she darted from podium to piece to place the proper cards around the rooms.

∞

He'd been able to quietly observe for more than an hour before Caroline found him again. Her surprise he was still in attendance was evident as she walked towards him with raised brows. "Well, what do you think so far?"

"It's good." He took a sip of champagne as she fell into step beside him.

Knowing this was as close to a compliment as the gallery would receive, she accepted it in kind. "I think so too. We've sold over half of the pieces so far, and I know it is not for sale, but you've received nine bids on 'Beautiful Fury' alone."

"Too bad it is *not* for sale."

She playfully swatted his arm. "I know, I just wanted you to know that it's appreciated and people love it. Not as much as I do, mind you. But they love it." She grinned as she started to slip away again.

"Where are you going?" He asked.

Turning towards him, she smiled. "I have to grab more sales tickets from my office. I'll be around." She started to walk away and then paused again. "Please don't leave."

He nodded that he would stick around and she hurried off. He walked up to a display shelf that housed 'Santa Fe Sunrise' and an older woman studied it as the rotating spotlight captured the piece at its rest and at its illumination state. She gasped as the piece came to life and then slowly faded away, and then gasped again as the light sent the piece into full radiance. "Have you ever seen anything like this?" she commented to Finn. "Absolutely astonishing work."

Not knowing how to respond, Finn just stood and watched her reaction change each time the shift in the piece occurred.

"I've been following F.W.'s career for several years now," she continued. "I don't understand how the Daulton managed to convince such an artist to showcase here." She began filling out a purchase ticket to take to Caroline. "I have to have it." She chuckled as she looked up at Finn. He offered a polite smile that she took as encouragement. "This piece will be great for my collection. The question will be which gallery to place it in."

"Gallery?" Finn asked.

She smiled up at him and nodded. "Yes. I own several galleries along the east coast. I love discovering new artists. F.W. does not sell much of his work. This is a good find."

"I see." Finn wasn't sure he liked the thought of his art floating from one gallery to the next. His pieces were personal, meant to be enjoyed on a personal level, not commercialized. He didn't want it sitting on a shelf in some gallery collecting dust, when it could be taken home and enjoyed every day by someone like Caroline. Rory had told him of her reaction to the piece.

"Where did Caroline run off to?" The woman began looking around and Finn slipped away to find Caroline before she did. He found her, discussing one of his vases with a woman dressed in gypsy style clothing, complete with bangled wrists and ankles. The vase suited the woman, and Finn listened as Caroline spoke of the process involved in creating a vase. She recounted the process with perfect clarity, though she did not speak about her personal experience, just the technique. "I've witnessed the artist at work and it is captivating to watch." She smiled at the woman and caught Finn's hesitant gaze over her head. She gently laid a hand on the woman's arm. "Excuse me a moment."

She hurried towards him. "You okay? Everything alright?"

"Listen," he whispered as he saw the art dealer from the east coast enter the atrium and spot Caroline. "'Santa Fe Sunrise' is not for sale." He had barely uttered the comment before the woman was embracing Caroline and gushing about the exhibit. *An old friend*, Finn realized, and knew his hopes of keeping the orbed sculpture were next to zilch.

He hurried away to catch his breath a moment before unleashing his rage on the woman for abusing his art. *She hadn't bought it yet*, he told himself. *Caroline would honor his wishes. Wouldn't she?* He ran a hand through his hair as he spotted Caroline walking towards the podium with the purchase ticket. He then watched as she walked a place holder over to the orb. Fuming, Finn stormed towards her.

He clasped a hand on her elbow. She didn't even jolt at his touch. "I told you it was not for sale. How dare you sell it to that woman." His voice was low and angry. She raised her even gaze up to his. "Calm down, Finn."

"No, I will not calm down." He began guiding her towards her office. "I specifically told you it was not for sale, and you sell it to some... some greedy woman who wants to just show it off instead of appreciate it."

"What are you talking about? I didn't sell it."

He looked down into Caroline's confused expression and then turned to look at the orb with the tidy place card sitting in front of it. "Then what do you call that?"

She patted his hand on her arm and began leading him back towards the piece. "Read it."

His eyes scanned the card and he immediately felt foolish. *Not for sale.*

"Oh."

She giggled softly under her breath and patted a reassuring hand over his arm. "Calm down, tiger." She winked at him as she started to walk away, but he gently tugged her hand to pull her back towards him. "Thank you." His relief evident. She was close, her hand in his, her other hand lightly resting on his arm. She moved the latter and placed it over his heart. "You're welcome." She felt the rapid pace beneath his suit. "Relax, I promise not to sell anything you wish to keep, okay?"

He nodded. "Thanks."

"Of course." She started to step away but he did not release her. "Finn," she spoke softly so as not to bring attention to him. "I have to go back to the atrium."

Reluctantly, he let his hands slip away and he nodded. She smiled as she squeezed his hand once more before heading into the other room.

"She is lovely," his mother's voice washed over him and set his nerves to sizzling as she linked her arm with his and laid her head against his shoulder. "You could only do worse."

"Mom," he warned under his breath.

"I'm just saying," she whispered back. "She's beautiful, smart, and loves art. Loves *your* art especially. She is friends with Rory, and most importantly," she turned to her son and brushed a delicate finger down his cheek. "She makes you smile."

"I am not dating Caroline, nor do I wish to. I do not want a relationship with her or anyone."

Sadness briefly flashed in his mother's eyes as she glanced towards Caroline and then back to him. "You deserve to be happy, Finnegan. And though I know you believe you can be happy alone, it's not true. You have too wonderful a heart to not share it with someone." She held a finger over his lips before he could interrupt. "Just think about it, sweetie." She kissed him on the cheek. "Your father and I are leaving now. We are going to check on Rosemary at the hospital before heading back to Taos." She hugged him once more. "We are so proud of you."

His dad walked up and hugged him as well. "Brilliant, Finn. Absolutely brilliant. I would have purchased every piece if your mother would have let me."

"Thanks, Dad." Finn smiled as he walked his parents to the door. "Give Rosemary a kiss for me."

"My pleasure." His mom's smile radiated love as excitement over seeing her new grandbaby washed over her. "Night, Sweetie. So proud of you," she called again as she walked away with his father. Enjoying the breeze on the sidewalk, Finn took a moment to inhale a few deep breaths before walking back inside. He'd almost reached his limit, and the thought of waiting it out in Caroline's office appealed to him more than walking around the gallery, but he wanted to see peoples' reactions, and if that meant mingling amongst them, he'd try to contain his anxiety a bit longer. His gaze caught Caroline's figure weaving through the crowd as she walked towards another sculpture and placed a card in front of it. Just the sight of her had his feet moving back into the gallery completely of their own volition.

«CHAPTER TWELVE»

Caroline slipped her feet out of her high heels and shuffled into her office. She tossed the shoes near her chair as she set the clipboard on her desktop. She then sat, rubbing her eyes as she braced herself for the paperwork that now lay before her. *It was a good sign*, she reminded herself. She looked to the small sculpture of 'Beautiful Fury' and ran a fingertip over it. A throat cleared and had her jumping in her seat. Finn leaned against the wall, arms crossed, waiting for her to notice him. "Finn!" She held a hand to her chest. "How long have you been in here?"

He glanced at his watch. "Too long. Is it over?"

A tired smile crossed her face and she nodded. "Yes. Everyone has gone home but me."

"And why have you not left yet?"

She waved her hand over her desk. "There's just a few things I would like to organize before the weekend, so that come Monday I can come in and immediately start shipping out pieces to their prospective buyers."

"You're tired, Caroline."

She shrugged.

"Go home. Start fresh on Monday."

Her brow perked. "Why, sure thing, Mr. Walsh. Yes sir." She chuckled and shook her head. "I really need to get a few things accomplished before calling it a night. You should feel proud though. This was the most successful exhibit in Daulton Gallery history."

It was his turn to shrug, and the lack of enthusiasm disappointed her.

"Well I thought it was a big deal," she murmured.

He smirked. "I am happy with how it went, I guess. I don't know what numbers you brought in, but I saw all the 'sold' signs out there, so that's a good sign. I appreciate it, Caroline. Rory will too."

She nodded. "So what has you lurking in my office, other than hiding from all the people?"

He blushed at her comment and she found the sight endearing. He rubbed a hand over the back of his neck. "I was waiting to see if you would like to go and— well— if you wanted to go and get a celebratory drink somewhere... or something."

Her heart skipped at his fumbled invitation and she softened at his awkwardness. "I would love to."

"But?" he added.

"No but. I would love to." She stood and slid her feet back into her heels. "You're right. This stuff can wait until Monday. We should go and celebrate."

"If you're too tired, I understand." The way she rushed about the room gathering her things had him nervously rethinking his invite.

"Not too tired." She smiled at him as she grabbed her keys. "Ready?" She watched as he stepped into the main hall towards the front doors and waited for her to set the alarm code. She shuffled him out the door and locked it behind them. Caroline tried to contain her excitement that Finn had actually asked to spend more time with her. She could already tell he hadn't meant to and was already questioning his request, but she would not give him time to back out of it. "Where to?"

"Somewhere quiet."

"I think I know the perfect place. We can walk if you want?"

"Sounds good."

They fell into a companionable silence. The sounds of local night owls enjoying the outdoor patios and live music drifted on the air. The scent of food teased her empty stomach. Caroline could not wait to ask him what he thought of the showcase, but she did not want to bombard him with questions just yet. They walked two blocks up the street and onto the back patio of a small margarita hut. "Will this work?"

Finn surveyed the small patio, and other than two other couples gracing tables, the place was empty. "Sure."

She sat at a bar top table and placed her purse in a vacant seat next to her. Finn sat across from her. She smiled in greeting at the waiter who swung by to take their drink orders.

"A beer," Finn said.

Caroline and the waiter exchanged looks. "Finn, it's a margarita place." she commented. "They only have margaritas."

Uncomfortable with the extra scrutiny of the waiter, he locked eyes with Caroline. "Whatever you're having then."

She ordered for the both of them and watched as the waiter hurried away. An awkward silence fell between them as she waited for Finn to speak, but he only sat, avoiding eye contact and looking seriously uncomfortable. *Small steps*, she told herself as she leaned forward. "So," she waited for him to turn towards her. "What made you decide not to sell 'Santa Fe Sunrise'?"

He crossed his arms in defense and Caroline inwardly sighed hoping he didn't close himself off from her.

"That woman was not the right person to have it."

"Renee Novice is one of the leading art collectors and dealers in the country."

"I don't care who she is. She wasn't the right person."

"Alright." Caroline held up her hands in surrender as the waiter slid their drinks onto the table and hurried away. Caroline bobbed her straw up and down to better mix her drink. "So what kind of person do you think should own such a piece?"

"Someone who appreciates it."

"Renee appreciated it."

"No, she didn't. She saw dollar signs and people gawking over it."

"Some would call that appreciation," Caroline pointed out.

"Not me."

"Obviously." There was no sting to her words, but she saw him shift in his chair as if to take flight any moment. "Okay, tell me this then, Finn." She took a sip of her drink before continuing. "In an ideal world, who would you pick as the perfect owner?"

He contemplated the question a moment. "You."

The answer was simple, and his answer serious. Her heart raced. "Me?" She took a moment to process his answer. "So does this mean you'll let me buy it?" she teased.

"No." He shook his head and her smile slowly faded. "Because I'm giving it to you."

Her eyes widened. "What?"

"It's yours. I designed it for you, therefore it should be yours."

"You designed it... for me?" Her breath caught and tears puddled in her eyes at the thought. "Why?"

Aggravated with himself for admitting it, Finn leaned back in his chair, his eyes hard. "I just did. We were sitting on the deck stairs and you asked me if I used my surroundings to inspire my art."

"I remember, but that was at sunset."

"So I took artistic liberties." Finn's lips quirked at that. "I wanted to capture that moment when the sun fades over the trees and filters through all the leaves. The bold colors of the sky and the speckles of filtered light just made sense. But it only came to fruition because I was designing for a specific person. So you should have it."

"Finn, I don't know what to say." She reached for his hand and he allowed her to take it, though he did not return the squeeze. "You've already given me a vase and the miniature 'Beautiful Fury,' I—"

"All designed for you."

Stunned, Caroline searched his face for meaning behind his words, but she could not read him. It wasn't until his words sunk in that she gripped his hand again. "'Beautiful Fury' was designed for me?"

"No. Sort of. No. Well, the miniature was. The original was designed for me, but you had a part in it." He tapped a finger on the back of her hand.

She didn't know what to say to that, so she changed the subject back to the other sculpture. "I have the orb priced at over—"

"I don't care," he interrupted. "It's a gift. Consider it a thank you gift if you want."

"Finn—"

He waved his hands to end the conversation. "Let's not talk about it anymore. It's yours. Done. Let's move on."

She bit back a smile as she retrieved her hand from his. "So how is Rory? I haven't been able to talk to her since the baby came."

Finn's shoulders relaxed as a lazy smile covered his face. "She's good. The baby is good. She's perfect." He paused a moment, reached into his pocket and pulled out his cell phone.

"Wow, I didn't know you had one of those." Caroline's sarcasm not going unnoticed, Finn grinned wickedly at her before opening up his photo album. He then laid the phone on the table and began scrolling through picture after picture of his new niece. Caroline watched him as he described her and described how his family reacted to the baby. "She's named Rosemary."

"That's beautiful." Caroline gazed at the sweet baby girl in the photograph. "It suits her."

"I think so too," he said proudly. "Rory and Dan are on cloud nine. My parents are having separation issues with her. Everyone has basically just lost their minds they're so happy."

"I can see that." She grinned at him as he looked up and he tried to mask his emotions but failed. "You can be excited, Finn. I think it's great."

He slid his phone back into his pocket. "They should be bringing her home from the hospital tomorrow."

"So you'll be back in Santa Fe again tomorrow?"

"I'm not leaving. I booked a hotel room for the night. I didn't feel like driving the hour and a half home."

"Smart."

"Where do you live?"

The question surprised her, but she pointed. "Just a few blocks up actually. There's a new building up the street that has a few lofts above the store fronts."

"You like living in the city?"

She shrugged. "It's convenient."

"I couldn't handle all the people."

"Why not?" Caroline didn't expect him to answer, but since he seemed talkative, well... talkative for Finn, she decided to go for it.

His brows rose at her question, as if surprised someone had the gumption to ask him. "I can't quite explain it. I've just never been one to like crowds. I was a bit of a loner in school. By choice," he added. "Other than my family, I never found a reason to really reach out to people. My family was enough. I didn't need anyone else. I had a few friends, but for the most part, it was Rory and me."

She quietly listened her heart squeezing at the thought of a life spent in such solitude. She couldn't imagine it. "I've always loved people," she admitted. "I like figuring out what makes them tick, what makes them who they are."

"And I could not care less." He paused a moment. "It sounds harsh and somewhat mean, and I don't mean for it to be... most of the time. I just don't like people knowing my business and assume other people feel the same way."

"But what if someone wants to get to know you? What then?"

"I don't know." The honesty in his quiet reply had a small smile tilting her lips.

"I'd like to think I have gotten to know you."

"Oh really? And what is it you know about me, Caroline? That I'm an artist." He leaned back and crossed his arms welcoming her assessment.

She grinned. "There is that. You value your privacy, but you also value your family. You would do anything for them, as is evident by the exhibition show for Rory. You're kind, even when you don't want or mean to be, as is evident by the miniature sculpture on my desk and the flowers you've given me in my vases. You are giving, which explains the 'Santa Fe Sunrise' sculpture you have gifted to me. You don't like crowds. You loathe someone invading your space and your workshop."

"And yet it doesn't stop you." He cut in making her laugh.

"You're patient, for the most part. You love what you do and it's evident in the way you do it. Not only does your art take patience, but you have incredible skill. And though you try to be tough and unapproachable, deep down you're a good guy with a kind heart."

He didn't respond and her cheeks flushed at his scrutiny. "So there you go," she ended by clasping her hands on the table. The waiter walked up and slipped the black folder containing their ticket onto the table. Finn grabbed it while Caroline's face was looking into her purse for her wallet. When she retrieved her credit card, the waiter was already walking away.

"My treat," he said.

She pointed to his glass. "You didn't even drink yours."

He shrugged and accepted the bill and signed his name. "Come on." He stood and extended his hand. "I'll walk you home."

She didn't tell him her car was still parked at the gallery. She didn't care that it was. She could walk over and get it tomorrow, because the fact that he wished to spend more time with her meant more than her car at the moment. She accepted his hand and allowed him to walk her down the sidewalk. He linked her hand through his elbow and stuffed his other hand into his pocket as they walked.

∞

"This is me."

She pointed to a red door and unlocked it. When she opened it, a flight of stairs led up to the second story and to her front door. Finn followed behind her, surprised that someone would want to live inside a tunnel. She unlocked her front door and flipped on a lamp. Finn hovered in the doorway, unsure of whether to follow her inside or to stay right where he was, exit in sight.

"Did you want to come in?" she asked, hanging her purse on the stand by the door.

He took a hesitant step inside and looked around. The room was cozy. Small, but cozy. She had a vibrant taste for color and the eclectic. And here and there he saw small pieces of art scattered and displayed. In an odd way, he felt relaxed amongst the cramped space. It smelled of her, all honey and vanilla, the scent he'd grown accustomed to over the last few months.

He walked a step further and noticed photographs on the wall. Family and friends smiled back at him, and he realized he didn't know much about her family. All he did notice was that none of the pictures were current. A smiling teenage Caroline stood by a woman that favored too closely not to be her mother, but it was the only photo he saw of the woman.

"That's my mom." She interrupted his line of thinking. "She died when I was seventeen."

"I'm sorry." His voice was gruff as he tried to comprehend such a loss. Caroline sighed beside him as she handed him a cold beer. "She was an amazing woman. An artist." She grinned at him as her eyes sparkled.

"Is that why you became an art gallery manager?"

She nodded. "I didn't have the gift of creating something from nothing, but I loved watching her work. So I decided I would take the task of showcasing such beauty."

"What kind of art did she create?"

"Mainly oil paintings. This is one of hers here." She pointed to the large landscape portrait hanging over her couch. "It's my favorite." The swirling brush strokes an ode to Van Gogh's technique, but the image a stunning creation all its own. The colors leapt off the canvas and Finn's fingers itched at the chance to somehow reimagine the painting in glass form.

"She was good."

"Yeah, she was." Caroline's voice quieted as she studied the piece a moment longer before turning to him.

"What about your dad?" Finn asked.

Surprise fluttered over her face that he continued to ask her questions, but she answered. "He's recently retired. He remarried a couple years after mom's death and now lives in Massachusetts. We never had much of a relationship, unfortunately, but he's happy and that's all that matters."

Finn saw the moment she grew uncomfortable with answering his questions and part of that pleased him. The woman of incessant questions did not like those questions turned on her.

"Do you see him much?" he asked.

"Not really. He and Veronica have two children together. They're in their teens so life is a bit busy for them."

Finn reached out and brushed a hand over the back of her hair as she stood still staring at her mother's painting. It felt like pure silk, and he took a cautious step away from her as he took a long sip of his drink. Caroline acted as if nothing had happened, *thankfully*, he realized, and continued her way to the kitchen. "Midnight snack?" she asked, pulling out some mini frozen pizzas.

The black, slinky dress that hugged her creamy skin, the meticulous make up she wore, the delicate silver necklace at her neck, none of that beauty appealed to him more than the fact she had reached into her freezer and pulled out frozen pizzas and had handed him a beer. He grinned. "Sure."

"I know it's not much, but they are pretty tasty despite the fact they are in a cardboard box." She poured several onto a plate and slid them into the microwave oven on the counter. She keyed in the time and hit the start button and then wiped her hands on a towel. When she turned to him, he was standing right next to her, his hand sliding over her cheek. His eyes focused on the shade of green that inspired 'Beautiful Fury', as he pressed his lips to hers. He had to give her credit, that despite her surprise, she did not pull away and punch him for making such a move. But all he knew was that in that moment of seeing her hold a box of mini pizzas with longing in her eyes for more time with the mother she adored and more time with a father she barely spoke to, he had to kiss her. He had to capture the sweetness she embodied, and he had to act on the feelings that had been confusing him over the last several months. He felt her hand lie gently against his chest as he guided his lips over hers, but he didn't pull away and neither did Caroline.

The beep of the microwave sounded and Caroline slowly backed away, resting her forehead against his, his hands still cupping her face. "Finn—" she paused a moment, the pulse in her neck matching the rapid rhythm of his own.

"I should go." His deep voice quieted as he released her.

"You don't have to leave." She reached for him but he was already retreating. He hurried towards the door and opened it. He turned, his eyes a storm of emotions as he took one last look at her and then rushed down the steps.

«CHAPTER THIRTEEN»

Come Monday, Caroline was back in her office and tallying up the total sales from Finn's exhibition show. Pleased with the results, she could not wait to tell Rory. She picked up the phone and dialed.

"If this is my favorite gallery manager calling with good news, then you have officially made my day." Rory's excited voice made Caroline laugh.

"I guess that would be me then."

Rory cheered on the other end and then sobered. "Okay, give me the details. Wait, first, I want to apologize again for not being there."

"You sort of have the best excuse possible," Caroline assured her.

"True." Rory's happiness flooded over the phone and into Caroline. "Second, my parents said Finn showed up. I am still in shock."

Caroline could not help but think of Finn and the kiss at her apartment. *Another perfect end to a perfect day*, she thought.

"Caroline?" Rory's voice echoed over the line.

"I'm here. Sorry about that."

"Were you just daydreaming about my brother?" Rory's teasing hit home though the younger sister did not know for certain.

"Very funny," Caroline retorted. "Speaking of your brother, though, I have yet to share the results with him."

"My word still stands. You can deliver him the results out at his place. In fact, if you wait until tomorrow, I will be over there with Rosemary and you can come see her too."

"Oh, I would love to see her!" Caroline pressed a hand over her heart at the thought of holding the precious baby.

"Then it's settled. Aim for lunch time. Dan and I are planning to cook out on Finn's deck."

"Alright, I will. It will probably take me that much time to get everything in order any way."

"So my mom said it was a spectacular night."

"It really was, Rory. And I cannot tell you how happy I was to see Finn walk in and get to witness it. He stuck around the entire time too!"

"Shut up! Really?"

"Well, he did hide in my office for a brief time, but yes, the entire time."

"Wow. I wonder what made him change his mind, other than seeing you."

Caroline's nervous laugh had Rory roaring. "I'm kidding! Sort of." She giggled.

"I think your sleep deprived mind is playing tricks on you, Rory Graves."

"Yeah, yeah, yeah."

Caroline could hear the soft cooings of Rosemary in the background and knew Rory must be holding her. "I can't wait to hold that precious girl of yours."

"She's pretty special. I am officially convinced she is the most beautiful baby in the world. Finn confirmed it as fact yesterday."

Caroline grinned at the sweet comment. "Well, I don't doubt it, and can't wait to witness her beauty for myself. But I should get back to work. I'll leave you in suspense on the results until tomorrow."

"Ugh, what am I supposed to do until then?" Rory whined and Rosemary whimpered loudly in the background. "Oh my goodness, I think I offended her."

Caroline laughed as Rory chuckled through the line. "Can't wait for tomorrow, Caroline. See you then!"

Caroline heard the click of the line and hung up. She then made her way to the stock room where Ed was boxing up the appropriate items and preparing them for shipping or pick up. She was excited about tomorrow as well. She hadn't heard from Finn since he left her apartment. She honestly didn't expect to either, until he decided when he wanted to see her again. *That's how he worked*, she realized. He needed space and time to think about the situation. Process it. Determine whether or not he had feelings for her. She understood that. *Then why did it aggravate her?* She sighed as she passed by 'Beautiful Fury.'

As she always did, she paused a moment to take in the sight. The blue, she realized, mirrored the color of Finn's eyes, that sharp blue that resided between cobalt and navy. In fact, the blue sculpture captured his personality perfectly. Raging one minute, yet soft and sweet along the edges closest to the green sculpture. Though the exterior edges were like blades down a dragon's back, the interior curves swerved, beautiful and smooth around the green silhouette. He'd mentioned she helped inspire the piece, but she couldn't quite figure out how. *Another time, Caroline*, she told herself. Eyeing the dramatic contrast a moment longer, she then continued on her way towards Ed.

∞

Rory watched as Caroline's car wound its way up Finn's driveway and her friend stepped out. She waved from the deck and Caroline returned the gesture before reaching into her back seat for gift bags and balloons. She made her way up the steps and smiled in greeting as Rory and Dan sat with her parents. Finn was nowhere to be found.

"Caroline!" Lyn stood up and walked towards her embracing her in a warm hug. "So good to see you."

Caroline beamed as she placed the anchored balloons on the patio table. "I come bearing gifts." She placed two bags on the side table next to Rory. "Some for baby girl." She reached into her purse and retrieved an envelope that sported the gallery's logo on the front. "And one for mom and dad. I also have one for Uncle Finn, but I guess he will just have to wait."

"He is currently showing Rosemary his workshop," Rory explained.

"Wow!" Caroline grinned. "Been alive less than a week and she's already allowed to enter the workshop? She needs to teach me her ways."

Rory laughed. "Tell me about it. He's already wrapped around her tiny finger."

"As are we all," Peter chimed in proudly as he stood to go check the grill.

Everyone looked up as Finn made his way carefully up his steps, the small pink bundle in his arms appearing as tiny as a fairy in his large embrace. His gaze caught Caroline and he paused a moment.

"Hello, Finn," she greeted, her gaze warming at the sight of him holding Rosemary.

"Caroline." He shuffled over towards Rory and handed the baby girl back to her mother. The reluctant tenderness made her heart swell.

"I brought your earnings from the show." She reached into her purse and pulled out the envelope.

He reached for it, his eyes connecting with hers and he paused. "Thanks." He shoved it into his back pocket and had her rolling her eyes.

"Aren't you going to open it?"

"I will later."

Rory tore into her envelope. "Well, I'm going to look at mine." Her jaw dropped as she gazed at the check inside. She found Caroline's gaze. "Is this for real?" Dan leaned over to look and started. Both looked to Caroline for approval.

"Yes. You have your brother to thank for negotiating that." She winked at Finn.

Rory and Dan looked at one another, both had tears brimming in their eyes as they hugged one another. "Finn," Rory stood, and carrying Rosemary towards Finn as she went, she wrapped her arm around his neck and kissed him soundly on the cheek. "Thank you, big brother," she whispered, as she laid her head against his chest. Finn accepted the hug by lightly patting her back and then brushing a fingertip down Rosemary's cheek.

"Don't mention it." He turned towards the grill where his father flipped burgers. Rory rolled her eyes at his back. She then swept Caroline into a huge hug. "This is incredible, Caroline. Thank you so much."

"I cannot take credit." She held up her hands as Lyn stepped towards her and hugged her again. "Yes you can, sweetie. The gallery looked beautiful. Finn's glass has never been displayed so well. I'm almost sad it couldn't look like that forever."

"It could if he accepted the offer in Angel Fire," Dan called out.

Caroline turned towards Finn. "What offer in Angel Fire?" Seeing Finn ignore the question, she turned towards Rory.

Proudly, his younger sister explained. "One of the resorts in Angel Fire wants to have a small gift shop that is just Finn's glass work. They have a few of his pieces in their lobbies and want to showcase him since he's a local. But naturally," she waved her hand towards her brother's back. "He's not interested. And he ignores me when I mention it!" Her voice rose so that it carried over towards Finn.

"I can't stand Angel Fire. Too many tourists," Finn explained, as he walked towards his patio door and disappeared inside. He emerged a few seconds later carrying a platter for his dad to set the finished burger patties on.

"What if you had a gallery in Santa Fe?" Rory asked. "Lots of local artists rent out a small space just to showcase their work."

"Santa Fe is too far."

"What about in Taos?" his mother added with a smile. "It's only about fifteen minutes away."

Feeling cornered, Finn shook his head and turned back to the grill.

"What about—"

"Don't press him. Let it be for now." Lyn warned Rory as she smiled towards Caroline. "Besides, right now we should be celebrating the wonderful show Caroline put on."

Caroline waved away the praise. "Please, let's not. I just came to see that baby." She reached towards Rory and Rory eased the little girl into Caroline's arms. "Caroline, meet Rosemary Finn Graves."

"Finn?" Caroline looked up and saw her friend nodding with a big smile. She then looked towards Finn's back. "He didn't tell me her middle name." She brushed a finger over the baby's small hand.

"He's still a bit embarrassed," Rory whispered under her breath and had Caroline smiling in complete understanding.

"It's not that I'm embarrassed," Finn turned an annoyed glance on the two women. "I just happen to like the name Rosemary and think that's the only name that's important."

"Right." Rory rolled her eyes but lovingly gazed upon her brother before looking down at her daughter in Caroline's arms. "Uncle Finn is full of it."

Laughing, Caroline watched as Finn's face flushed before he turned to accept a beer from Dan.

"Please say you are staying to eat with us?" Lyn asked.

Rory nodded. "I invited her." She directed a firm glance towards her brother's surprised expression. Brooking no argument, she smiled and turned back to an aloof Caroline as her friend fawned over Rosemary. "Yes ma'am," she replied. "Though," she glanced up towards Finn, "I do need to talk shop with you for a few minutes."

"Now?"

"Whenever," she shrugged. "Just need to before I leave."

"Let's do it now."

Caroline handed Rosemary back to Rory. "I'll be back. I'm not done holding that little cutie."

Rory grinned and waved her away as Caroline pulled Finn by the elbow down the deck stairs for more privacy.

"So, what is so important?" he asked as they walked towards his shop. Her hand had not left the crook of his elbow and he felt he was completely fine with escorting her across the yard. He tried to calculate how many miles he'd walked the well-worn path between his house and his shop. *Too many to count*, he realized, and the thought warmed him. He loved where he lived. Loved it as a kid, but did not really appreciate it until he was older. The trees and flowers imparted their scent on the air around him and relaxed him. Much of his art was inspired by just existing in this particular spot. His house, with the view of mountains and trees, captivated him on a daily basis with nature's beautiful backdrop.

"I have had more than six galleries across the country contact me in regards to your work," Caroline began, gauging his reaction, and then paused. "Finn, this is exciting!" She released his arm and stepped in front of him.

"Let me guess, Renee Novice?" he asked, shifting his attention from his surroundings to the woman beside him.

"She's one of them, yes."

He rolled his eyes.

"But not all of them are like her," Caroline defended, still not realizing why Finn disliked the woman so much. "One is a small but prominent gallery in Portland, another is in Mobile, Alabama, and then there's—"

"I'm not interested, Caroline." He cut her off but without sting.

"They've emailed me information, Finn. I can get it to you to look over. What some of these galleries offer makes the Daulton look like chump change."

"Still not interested."

Sighing, she nodded. "I understand. Well, I will pass the messages along to Rory any way, since she's your representative."

"That's fine." He reached for her hand and linked it back around the crook of his elbow as they turned to make their way back towards the house.

"I wasn't sure if I would hear from you or not, so that is why Rory told me to bring by the payments today. I hope I'm not intruding." Caroline looked up at him and he shook his head.

"You would have heard from me."

"Well, I know I would have eventually, I just didn't know if—"

"Hey you two!" Rory called from over the deck railing. "Burgers are ready!"

For once, Finn was actually thankful for his sister's interruption. The remaining portion of their conversation would have to wait. He wasn't quite ready to talk about his feelings about Caroline much less *with* Caroline. He knew it was inevitable, but he just needed a bit more time to figure some things out. He wasn't sure if he was ready for a relationship, for one. Granted that was all pending on whether or not she wanted one too. He assumed she did, but he wasn't sure if that was his male ego talking or if she did indeed have feelings for him. He didn't exactly give her a chance to say anything after he kissed her. *And this was the reason why*, he scolded himself. Because he did not want to face rejection from her, and he didn't want to be talking to himself while standing next to the woman. Annoyed with himself, he kept his current thoughts quiet.

∞

They reached the deck and Caroline accepted the plate from Lyn and the burger from Dan. She then walked over to the table to add all the fixings, as Finn stood right next to her decking his own burger. He stood so close, she could smell the soap on his skin. Her nerves hummed at the memory of him kissing her in the kitchen and the way he'd smelled then too. *He'd worn cologne*, she realized, as his scent was different that night. But the underlying hint of Finn was still there. He bumped her elbow and she dropped the mustard. She quickly grabbed the spinning bottle and steadied her hands. Rory watched like a hawk as her brother awkwardly reached across Caroline and fumbled his own slice of cheese. She grinned as the two tried every way in the world to physically avoid one another. Laughing to herself, she cradled Rosemary closer for protection.

Knowing neither one would kill her as she held such innocence. The last fumbled bread bun from Caroline had Rory hooting in laughter. "Oh my goodness, you guys! You're killing me!"

Caroline and Finn glanced up as all eyes were on them.

"Did you two kiss again?"

Both sets of cheeks flushed with the accusation and Caroline turned towards the stairs. But Finn placed a restrictive hand on her arm. She scrambled the plate in her hands as he released her and he took it from her. He set both plates on the table and eyed her cautiously.

Finn's mother's face broke into a broad smile of pleasure at the idea of her son and Caroline.

Dan and Peter just laughed at Rory's sheer delight at the expense of her brother's embarrassment.

"That is not your concern, Rory." Finn's voice was cool and surprisingly calm as Caroline wished she could just disappear and slowly slink away. Rory looked to Caroline and burst into laughter all over again. "Caroline, you could not look any guiltier than a teenage boy after curfew."

Sputtering, Caroline tried to think of something to say as Lyn linked her arm with hers and patted her hand. She winked at her son. "Come now, Caroline, just come sit and eat, sweetie."

She grabbed Caroline's plate and shot a warning glance at Rory not to screw this up for Finn, but Rory eyed her brother with curiosity. "I'm going to take that as a yes." She beamed up at him as he tousled her hair before grabbing his own plate and sitting beside her. "Mind your own business, Ro."

Slowly, the awkward moment passed and Caroline began to finally relax again, except when she would notice Finn looking her direction. She'd divert her gaze and try to focus on the conversation around her. She felt clumsy under his scrutiny and she wondered what he was thinking. As was typical of Finn, she had not heard from him since he left her apartment. He said he would have contacted her eventually, but would he have mentioned the kiss? Or would it be like last time and they not talk about it? Confused, Caroline finished the last bite of her burger and tried to create a convincing excuse to depart so soon after eating. She came up empty.

Rory slid into the seat beside her and draped her arm around her shoulders. Rosemary now resided comfortably in her daddy's arms and Rory leaned forward to snatch a cookie off of her mother's plate. "So, when did it happen?" Rory asked quietly. Lyn swatted her thigh but leaned in closer so as to be included in the conversation.

Caroline's face deepened in color as she took a sip of her drink. "I really don't want to talk about it."

"Was it in your office the night of the exhibition?"

"No, don't be ridiculous," Caroline whispered.

"Then when?"

"He walked me home."

Rory and Lyn exchanged a look of excitement. "He walked you home? Did you not drive to the gallery?"

"I did, but we went for drinks afterward and it wasn't far from my loft."

"You went for drinks?" Rory rubbed her palms together and Caroline stifled a laugh even though she was still embarrassed by the line of questioning.

"His idea or yours?" Lyn asked and then shrugged as if she didn't care that she was Finn's mom asking the question.

"Umm, his," Caroline replied and had both women squealing. She tried to shush their outburst, but when she caught Finn's eye she wished she could disappear.

He stood and walked towards the women. "I think we need to talk." He extended a hand towards Caroline and she nervously accepted it rising to her feet.

Rory spanked her rear as she shuffled away from the table. Caroline spun to catch the quick wink Rory sent her way as Finn escorted Caroline into the house. He pointed to his couch. "Have a seat."

∞

She eased onto the leather sofa and braced herself for whatever rejection or harshness he intended to throw her way. Instead, he sat beside her and ran a hand over his face. "So," he sighed. "I have something I need to run by you."

Caroline took a cautious breath. "Okay..."

"I want to open a small gallery in Santa Fe."

Flabbergasted this was the immediate topic of conversation, she turned to him. "What?"

"I think you heard me." He smiled briefly as she groped for understanding.

"But you said you weren't interested and that Santa Fe was too far."

"I wasn't entirely lying." He leaned forward, resting his elbows on his knees and looked through the glass windows towards the patio where his family sat.

"I'm not going to lie, Finn, I'm a bit confused."

He flashed a quick, devastating grin. "I thought you might be."

Caroline tampered down her impatience. "Care to explain then."

"Rory is a mom now. She needs a stable income. Her running all over the city trying to make deals for artists is not good for her or the baby. If she had a gallery to run then she'd only have one client and one focus. It would be in town, so she would not have to travel."

"So you want to open a gallery so that your sister will have a job?"

"Not only that." He rubbed a hand over the back of his neck before turning towards her. "Listen, the night of the exhibition I was at a loss. I never imagined my work being showcased like that before. Call it fear, call it pride, call it ignorance, I don't care. I just never imagined it possible. Seeing it displayed was... well, it was really something."

A soft smile crossed her face and he reached for her hand. "And I know that is your doing. But it made me think about the future. And no, I don't want to have my work shipped to different galleries across the country. But to have a small place to sell my work is smart, in terms of business. It also allows me the opportunity to keep creating. Rory has hounded me for years to stop hoarding my glass, and maybe she's right. And now, with Rosemary, I want Rory to be able to focus on raising her. I don't want her to ever stress about whether or not one client's work is selling or not. I want her to be able to work a somewhat more stable job than that. And I think my glass can do that." He waited to see what Caroline said. If she thought his wild idea was even possible.

"Do you have any idea where you would open up the gallery?"

"I didn't until I walked you home the other night."

"What?"

"Your loft. It sits above store fronts. I noticed the one next to you was for rent. It's in the perfect spot. Still close enough to Canyon Road to attract art hoppers, but far enough away that it's not lumped into all the galleries. It's also part of an active retail strip, so shopping traffic will be in the area."

"You've really thought about this." Caroline felt his excitement, and she also felt his eagerness.

"Yeah. I have."

"And have you asked Rory if this would be something she would even want to do?"

"Not yet. I was sort of hoping to just do it, and then give it to her."

Caroline grimaced and his eyes widened. "You don't think that's a good idea."

"Absolutely not." Caroline muffled a laugh at his wounded expression. "It's a sweet idea, Finn."

She saw him begin to retreat and she gripped his hand. "No, don't bail on me now, Finnegan. Let me explain."

He eyed their linked hands and then looked at her, liking the way his full name sounded rolling off her tongue. "I think, because Rory has Rosemary to think about now, that you should present the idea to her. You don't want to make decisions for her or coerce her into a decision. Rory is too strong-headed for that."

Sighing, he leaned back against the cushions. "You're right."

"But I think it is a great idea." Caroline smiled. "If I weren't happy at the Daulton I would offer to help get it started."

"Will you help her though, if she has any questions?"

"Of course I will." Caroline felt his grip tighten and he lifted her hand and kissed the back of it.

"Thanks."

Caroline nodded. She tugged her hand free and patted her thighs before standing. "Well, I guess I should head back. It's a bit of a drive back to Santa Fe."

"You're welcome to stay."

"Excuse me?" She turned and his face flushed.

"I meant... stay longer. You don't have to rush off."

"That's okay. I think you guys should enjoy family time without me butting in." She looked at his cell phone on the coffee table in front of him. "So since I listened to your secret plan, and you may need my help in the future, don't you think it's about time we exchange phone numbers?" She tilted her head towards his phone.

"But then how would I avoid you?"

His comment had her laughing and he grinned.

"Very true. And since that seems to happen quite a bit, I'll just retract the question."

Finn walked towards her and handed her his phone. "Put your number in."

"Really?" she asked.

"Yes. Besides I've been thinking about something else too."

"And what's that?" She didn't look up as she created a new contact in his phone and added her information.

"That maybe I don't want to avoid you."

She looked up. "What?" Her breath caught as he stepped closer and slipped his phone out of her hands and into his pocket. He felt her pulse jump under his fingertips as he held her hands in his.

"Look, I'm not good at this and to be honest I'm pretty new at it... But I'd like to talk to you more." His words trailed off as he struggled with how to word his feelings.

"That's what I'm saying," Caroline interrupted, reaching for her own phone. "That's why we are exchanging numbers." She held her phone towards him and he shook his head.

"That's not what I'm talking about."

She waited and he growled in frustration. "Okay," He pulled her back towards the couch and nudged her to sit. He sat next to her and rubbed one of his hands over his mouth. "Here it is." He took a deep breath and Caroline watched him with confused green eyes. "When I designed 'Beautiful Fury' it was meant to be for you."

"Me?" she asked quietly. "But I thought the miniature was just meant for me.

"No. I designed the original with you in mind. That day, after the farmer's market when you drove me completely nuts, I went into my shop and just exploded. Something in me just poured into the glass. I felt—" he held his hands to his chest as if to pull his meaning from within. "I felt like I had met my match. I was so irritated at you. Irritated that you could get under my skin and make me want—"

Rory's head popped in the patio door. "Hey guys, mom and dad are leaving."

"Get out, Rory!" Finn barked.

Rory's eyes widened but she immediately darted back out the door.

"Finn," Caroline scolded and started to stand to go and apologize to Rory. He tugged on her hands to keep her in place.

"She'll be fine. Look, if I don't say this now then I won't have the nerve later and then I *will* avoid you."

She inhaled and waited. He knew he was trying her patience, he was trying his own, but he wanted to make sure he got this right.

"You're the green sculpture." He blurted it out fast so as not to chicken out, and by the look on her face he still had some explaining to do. "I'm the blue." He scooted closer towards her and she backed away slightly, the move causing his chest to tighten. "Look, the green is the same color as your eyes. I did that on purpose, Caroline. You were the calm amidst my turmoil. And yet, no matter how hard I tried to despise you, I couldn't. Hence, the blue." He pointed at himself. "I rage against you and you take it in stride. Other than Rory, no one has ever done that with me."

She sat so still and quiet he feared he'd scared her.

"Do you understand me now?"

She lightly fingered the necklace at her throat. "I, uh, think I am beginning to. 'Beautiful Fury' is us?"

"Yes." He nodded, a brief smile covering his face until he saw she didn't return it. "I've freaked you out." He backed away and released her other hand.

"No, Finn, wait—" But he was already out the door. Jumping to her feet she chased him out of the house as he barreled his way past his parents and sister towards his workshop. "Finn!" She called after him as she too raced down the steps. She caught him around the arm and pulled him to a stop. "Wait a minute." Breathless, she studied him a moment. She gently cupped his face. "I understand what you are telling me." She smiled tenderly at him and slowly felt him begin to relax. "I don't want to avoid you either."

His lips twitched at that statement and he leaned his forehead against hers. A long moment of silence passed between them, but instead of feeling uncomfortable, for once, he felt at ease. "I'm glad." He exhaled a deep breath of relief that had her smiling.

Wrapping her arms around his neck, she felt his lips graze her forehead. The sound of Rory's cheering in the background had them both stopping and huddling together in embarrassment. "If I could kill her, I would," Finn whispered and had Caroline throwing her head back in laughter.

"Oh, but then who would run your gallery?" She beamed up at him as he unwound her arms from around his neck and linked hands with her. He flashed a handsome grin and winked. "I have a back-up plan."

«EPILOGUE»

Three months later...

Rory settled Rosemary's carrier into one of the extra chairs and sighed. "I swear, for three months old she is a hefty little thing." Her mother and Caroline found their own seats at a small table on Frank's patio and smiled at the sweet baby girl who only grinned and gurgled up at her mother. "I still cannot believe you are dating my brother," she added as Matilda waved to them, then hustled menu's over and hurried back towards the counter to cash out other customers.

"I don't want to talk about it."

"That bad, huh?" Rory asked and received looks of exasperation from the other two women. She grinned.

"No, I just do not want to talk about it."

"Is that because Finn threatened to kill you if you did?"

"Pretty much."

Rory laughed. "Wow, my brother the romantic."

"Now Rory," Lyn began. "Your brother is a complex man."

"Oh, Mom, please." Rory rolled her eyes and had Caroline chuckling. "He's like a whole new man, Caroline."

"Really? How so?"

"I dropped by his house yesterday and walked right into his workshop. He didn't even yell at me."

"Did you have Rosemary with you?" Caroline asked, pointing out the obvious reason why Finn would not lash out.

"Oh." Rory nodded. "That's why. Wow, she's a great buffer, isn't she?" She lightly tapped a finger to her little girl's nose. "Between you and Rosemary, Finn is almost... dare I say, friendly."

"We aim to please. Isn't that right, Rosemary?" Caroline rubbed a hand over the downy dark hair and then straightened the small pink headband.

A buzz sounded through the air and Caroline glanced at her phone. A smile split her face as she reached for it.

"Uh oh, it's him, isn't it?"

"Shhh," Caroline answered with a grin. "Hey, Finn."

The other two women watched in awe as they heard a muffled voice on the other end and joy radiated from Caroline. The fact that Finn's side of the conversation seemed more than two words long was impressive enough, but the glow on Caroline's face spoke volumes more as to her feelings for Finn. She hung up and sighed.

"And how is my big brother?" Rory asked.

"Good. He's going to stop by the Daulton after lunch. He's currently at his gallery."

"Is he now?" Lyn asked with a raised brow. "He specifically told me not to bother him today because he would be working in his shop."

"Oh, well technically he is. Just a different shop," Caroline added in his defense, making the other two women smile and tease her. She waved their mocking gestures aside as her phone rang again. "I'm sorry." She saw it was Finn again.

"Yes?"

Her smile faded and she bolted to her feet and gathered her purse. "I'm on my way." Hanging up, she looked to the other two ladies. "I'm sorry, I have to go."

"What's going on?" Rory asked, worry etching her face as Caroline hurried to leave.

"He's dealing with the painters and it's not going well. Finn's about ready to snap. I'm going over to the new gallery to run interference for a bit while he steps out to take a breather. So sorry to be bailing on our lunch plans."

"No apology necessary, dear." Lyn waved her away as they both watched Caroline hurry down the sidewalk.

"Keep us updated!" Rory called after her and received an over the shoulder wave in acknowledgement.

"She's a good fit for him." Lyn said. "She cares for him and understands his needs."

Rory nodded. "I agree. Though I still do not know how she deals with Finn's temperamental moods."

"The same way we do, sweetie... with love."

∞

Caroline walked up to Finn's gallery and paused as she saw him sitting on the curb outside the front. She rushed towards him and sat, her hand on his back. "You okay?"

"I'm fine." He tossed aside the small branch that was in his fist. "For the life of me, I have tried being nice."

Caroline shot a look towards the men inside, all of them anxiously awaiting Finn's return. "What happened?"

"They just aren't understanding me. Or it could be I'm a perfectionist."

"That's probably it." She smiled as he shrugged at his own annoyance.

"Want me to go whip them into shape?"

He shook his head. "No. I just needed a breather and to see you." He kissed her hand. "Thanks for coming."

"Always." She smiled as he stood and pulled her to her feet as well.

"Want to come see the progress?"

"Sure." He rose to his feet and helped her stand as well. Walking inside, she gasped. On the back wall, the glass display case housed only one piece.

'Beautiful Fury,' along with his original sketches of the design.

"You already moved it?" She asked, eyeing her favorite sculpture.

He grinned. "It's inspiration."

She kissed his cheek as she watched the painters continue their work. "So what's the problem with the painting?" She asked. "Everything looks fine."

Finn shook his head. "Everything in this room looks fine. It's this side room that is a disaster." He walked in front of her as he led the way. "I hired an extra artist to help, but they still seem confused on what it is I actually want."

He flicked the light and Caroline froze. She covered her mouth with both her hands as a sob escaped through. On the dominant wall of the room, a mural painted as an exact replica of her mother's painting she housed upstairs in her loft graced the wall. Tears clouded her vision as she studied the gorgeous artistry. The broad strokes of bright color brought the room to life. "I have some great ideas for this room." Finn's voice echoed in the empty space as he waited for Caroline to turn around.

Swiping away happy tears she turned and threw her arms around him. She tried to bite back another sob and ended up snorting. She laughed nervously as he grinned. "I can't believe this, Finn." She swiped at her cheeks as he held her in his arms.

"Six months ago you walked into my workshop with the purpose of making me a better artist." He reached for her trembling hands and kissed them. "Little did I know that you would make me a better person. Like 'Beautiful Fury', you are the calm and I'm the storm. I am like my glass, Caroline, and you are the fire. You've refined me into something new. I don't know how you put up with me, but I'm thankful you do." He paused a moment to smile and look into her tear stained face. "Since meeting you, Caroline, my plans of solitude shifted. Slowly you wound your way into my life and eventually right into my heart. I love..." his voice broke as he cleared his throat. "I love you, Caroline, and this room is in honor of you."

She jumped into his arms and hugged him close as her eyes soaked in the image of her mother's painting over his shoulder. She wondered what artist he hired to complete such a massive project. Though it was not painted in oils, the mural was as close to the original as it could be. She looked to the bottom right corner of the wall where a date was scrawled, and there she found two small initials. 'F.W.'

She gasped and pulled far enough away from Finn's face to hold it in her hands. "You painted this." She searched his face and kissed him. "This is one of your best gifts yet." She kissed him again and smiled against his lips. "I love you too, Finnegan Walsh. Always."

**All titles by Katharine E. Hamilton
Available on Amazon and Amazon Kindle**

The Unfading Lands
https://www.amazon.com/dp/B00VKWKPES

Darkness Divided, Part Two in
The Unfading Lands Series
https://www.amazon.com/dp/B015QFTAXG

Redemption Rising, Part Three in
The Unfading Lands Series
https://www.amazon.com/dp/B01G5NYSEO

Chicago's Best
The Lighthearted Collection
https://www.amazon.com/dp/B06XH7Y3MF

Montgomery House
The Lighthearted Collection
https://www.amazon.com/dp/B073T1SVCN

Find out more about Katharine and her works at:
www.katharinehamilton.com

Social Media is a great way to connect with Katharine. Check her out on the following:

Facebook: Katharine E. Hamilton
https://www.facebook.com/Katharine-E-Hamilton-282475125097433/

Twitter: @AuthorKatharine
Instagram: @AuthorKatharine

Contact Katharine:
khamiltonauthor@gmail.com

ABOUT THE AUTHOR

Katharine E. Hamilton started her writing career a decade ago by creating fun-filled stories that have taken children on imaginative adventures all around the world. Katharine now extends the invitation to adults everywhere. She finds herself drawn time and again by the people behind her adventures and wishes to bring them to life in her stories.

She was born and raised in the state of Texas, where she currently resides on a ranch in the heart of brush country with her husband, Brad, and their son, Everett, and their two furry friends, Tulip and Cash. She is a graduate of Texas A&M University, where she received a Bachelor's degree in History.

She is thankful to her readers for allowing her the privilege to turn her dreams into a new adventure for us all.

CPSIA information can be obtained
at www.ICGtesting.com
Printed in the USA
LVHW092248310320
651840LV00003B/488

9 780692 068250